Time is the
Longest
Distance

Time is the Longest Distance

Larry Fondation

Published by Raw Dog Screaming Press
Bowie, MD

First Edition

Cover Image: Larry Fondation
Book Design: Kevin Kusisto

Printed in the United States of America

ISBN: 9781947879010

Library of Congress Control Number: 2017961594

www.RawDogScreaming.com

For Rinnie

Also by Larry Fondation

Common Criminals: L.A. Crime Stories

Angry Nights

Fish, Soap and Bonds

Unintended Consequences

Martyrs and Holymen

Acknowledgements

Grateful acknowledgement to the following publications in which some portions of this novel have previously appeared: *The Industrial Worker Book Review - The Fiction Issue*; *Numero Cing* (Canada); and *Prism Review*.

Contents

"I didn't go to the moon, I went much further – for time is the longest distance between two places."

Tennessee Williams, *The Glass Menagerie*

"Time is the substance I am made of. Time is a river which sweeps me along, but I am the river; it is a tiger which destroys me, but I am the tiger; it is a fire which consumes me, but I am the fire."

Jorge Luis Borges, *Labyrinths: Selected Stories and Other Writings*

"Time present and time past
Are both perhaps present in time future,
And time future contained in time past.
If all time is eternally present
All time is unredeemable."

T.S. Eliot, Burnt Norton, *The Four Quartets*

Introductory Rites

Prelude to Time is the Longest Distance

I am looking for a blue thread and I am looking for my Bekah. That is what this is about.

I have a lucky quarter, too, and that quarter may help me. My mother gave it to me when I was little, and that was some time ago. I'm not sure how long ago. I have my doubts about time.

I was a student and then I was not. Writing about Hawthorne and Nathanael West. My favorite Americans. Then I found crime and then I found dirt and I found San Julian Street and cardboard boxes to sleep in and Albert and Joey and sometimes Bekah and I remembered lingonberries and pawn shops and D'Wayne preaching on the sidewalk and I found air and light and grime and matter and I began to wonder all the time and to think about the thoughts between my thoughts and about witches and memorials and about the heavy metal grates and the noises of stores opening for business in the morning, in Los Angeles, east of Main Street, east of San Pedro and down by the River, where once there was nothing and then there were tents and boxes alive and we were all there and now there is something else altogether and soon there will be something else because all endings have beginnings and all beginnings have endings and then something begins again. And this is me and this is Albert and this is another and another, all atoms and matter, and this is Bekah, always Bekah. In the beginning was the Word, just not this word, these words, no signs or symbols everlasting, no ideas but in things, or in persons, just that quarter and the blue thread and my Bekah, and maybe Albert and perhaps Joey and the wisteria and the smell of jacaranda in the Springtime months, and the heavy air of our times, and the fires and the floods and the winds. And always the River.

Los Angeles is not a first chance or a second chance or even another throw of the dice. Los Angeles is rehab, a fourth chance or a fifth. Sometimes we fail them all. Sometimes not. Fall seven times; get up eight. Sometimes you can only crawl. And sometimes crawling is good enough.

Nine times out of ten, I am crawling.

I have to put a circle around this beast.

As a kid, we had roast beef on Sundays when my Dad was working; we had Kraft Mac and Cheese when he was not.

I can see clearly now; tomorrow will not be so good.

I think this is what it's like.

I see doorways and steel grates; pigeons and vomit; treasures and detritus; Hawthorne in Salem and the inside of my own mind; cigarette butts and Coke cans—discarded and disused; debris and refuse; things left behind; I see the Holy Spirit, sometimes better than most; I see mice and and spiders and roaches; I admire the work of ants; I keep my eyes—and my body—quite close to the ground.

Out of the Tent

Out of the tent, then back in again. Avoid sunlight. Inside, outside. Cops come, then leave, then come back.

Other perspective: In his doorway, the bum stirred. Flies buzzed around him as they do around a dump. The morning sun was bright as a cop's flashlight.

The storeowner kicked him.

"You gotta move. I gotta get in."

Albert moved his shit out of the way. He packed his blankets and all his belongings in his shopping cart. The cart said "Von's."

With Albert gone, the businessman opened his store.

* *

Later on, someone stole his shopping cart while he was sleeping. Lucky he had his blankets and all his warm clothes wrapped tightly around him. But it takes him a week to get another cart.

* *

SLEEPING
IN
DOORWAYS.
SIDEWALKS.
TENTS.
BOXES.

IN THE ALLEY.
BY THE DUMPSTER.
LATE AT NIGHT.
SHE: DIRTY, BITTEN NAILS.

THEY FUCK.

INSIDE
OUR
TENT,
PITCHED
ON
THE
SIDEWALK.

HOLDING
HANDS
IN
LINE
AT
THE
SOUP
KITCHEN.

* *

All things happen at once. There is no time.

Shortly after I'd been accepted into the PhD program, the doctor told me I was losing my mind. I'd been acting weird so I went to find out why.

You want to hear about jellyfish? I can still remember, though it doesn't all come together for me anymore.

As an undergraduate, I majored in biology, with an emphasis on oceanography. I studied jellyfish, drifters, all things buffeted about in the sea. As a senior, I discovered literature.

I was feeling weird. A lot. I went to the doctor. He said I was losing my mind. I forget what he said. Something about meds. Something. I walked out the door.

I went to the doctor. He said I was fine.

Different versions—same story.

I'm always thinking.

* *

How casually we toss off a life—stepping on ants as we go on, swatting small bugs that happen to alight on the skin of our bare forearm.

Los Angeles Witch Trials

The witch trials in Los Angeles began in the summer of 2005. They said Rebecca was hearing voices, screaming at all hours. Some of the ministers stuck up for us; others said we were whiskey-drinkers, drug-takers and evil-doers.

The hotels started to change. New coats of paint. New people.

In the morning, they picked off the easy ones—Sarah Good and Sarah Osborne and Tituba, beggars and outcasts, all of them. Arraignments occurred in Corwin's court. Drug possession, and petty theft and public drunkenness, and vagrancy—rounded up and deposited, cells full and beds barred, hospitals unattainable.

What crime is mine? Corey asked.

Wizards and buzzards and projections of refracted light cast upon the courtroom ceiling. Thirty days, sixty days, nothing really—but disruption. Disarray, discontent, disturbance. My tent, our tent, our boxes, without neighbors, absent and attenuated, "Order in the court." Bedlam and mayhem, undischarged.

First results: Corey, Viet. Vet, prosecuted harder, reasons unknown, pressed into labor, clear the fallen rock. Appeal from Muni Court—one up, Superior. Next up: Hathorne presiding: No change, verdict upheld—"Highway maintenance—the inmates from San Julian." Hollywood Holiday Inn—orange vests and trash bins—vagrants, vagabonds.

Next complaint: outlaw sleeping in public places. Poverty per se a criminal act. Putnam wants my property. Revitalize the neighborhood. Gilmore, smiling, wants my place. One of the good guys. Prosecution and court appearance, nonetheless. Dueling ministers, both named Mather. The aforenamed, name of my grade school. Truly. One talks compassion. Noblesse oblige, if I remember my studies accurately. The other —Malleus Maleficarum. The lesser of two evils, or the banality of evil, I can't remember which. Testimonies as chatter, white noise. Mohammed Atta bought his plane ticket under his own name. Fuck the notion of nom de plume.

Perhaps we are national security risks now, never, nonetheless. Hale to the chief! Straight out of Beverly. Updike the only Marblehead man I know, wearing madras plaid pants, Martha's Vineyard. 'Ata boy, mate!

Unsettled baton—debased rights. Spectral crescent moons. Diadat Lawson is my favorite name.

Back to court —— and spark. Sherbet T—shirt stockings. Los Angeles is my platinum blonde, my forever love, five inch spike heels striking pavement in 5:4 time. Paul Motian, my next favorite name. Doo—doo—da—da—doot. Et cetera.

Next up, the nurse of Skid Row. Spectral has been my forte—my dirty secret: I saw the minister's veil, countenance undisclosed. I never liked the trees, the woods, not at night, not in day, gatherings ungathered, undismayed.

Sentences handed down, by whose floating hands, unfloating: 90 days community service—trash clean-up, a week at Sybil Brand.

Trials resume. Time lost.

New evidentiary rules introduced –

    Condominiums converted

    City Council Resolutions

    Parking meters installed, new fees imposed.

    Exile—5th St., 6th St., Los Angeles, San Julian, Wall Street.

> Situational support

Corner café.

Digression: Back to trials—"Rid the area. Scourge. Purge the poison. Neanderthal. Not human."

Homo sapiens, sapiens displaced less than thirty thousand years ago. The New World is everywhere except Africa. We have never left home, domiciles notwithstanding.

Testimonies abound. We are all at the mercy.

The judge recesses for lunch.

Jackhammers struck;
The building came down –
In bits and pieces,
Then all at once.
Our candles and lights,
Crushed all at once –
Piles of stuff,
Gathered then scattered,
All gone, but no matter –
Here and there,
All over –
She and I,
She and I.

* *

Bekah says:

I think they think it's good
When they raze the building we live in,
Brick by brick,
Board by board,
But we have nowhere, nowhere to go,
But it's OK,
We have no rent to pay.

Begging. Asking. Asking questions. Asking for money. Beg the question. Beg for money. Mendicancy. Beggar. Baker. Candlemaker. Thief. Gandhi in rags. Alms. Begging for alms. Asking for alms. What are alms? Are you asking for help? Help?

What? No. Signs of brown cardboard, lettered with Sharpies. Black, but sometimes, blue or red. Is washing windows work? Antonio and Jan and the Central City Association. On the corner with NBC, ABC, CNN, all the above, alphabet soup, but just for this one day, one day, this one day only. Not me. Every day. Asking. Asking ultimate questions: A dollar. A quarter. A song on the radio. A Siren. A siren. Is it raining? I have no Suitors. I have Omensetter's Luck.

The birds flew up and over us some place:

Rubble strewn on desktops;

Broken coffee,

Torn tea and trash.

Leaves eat the sun and the air.

Scattered sheets of glass,

Shattered, then reformed.

We come from ice.

* *

Scrap and detritus are my substance,
Jackhammers cracking concrete,
    Carving out letters,
    Cutting asphalt,
    Spelling out words.
Beetles face off on the curbstone,
Screaming war cries,
Ants burdened by armor and ammunition.

Mud and rain and plant parts…

They were replacing the parking meters on San Pedro.

Parking meters replaced. Without head. Stems in the ground. Stuff the stems like time capsules. Hurry before they put the money changers on top. The place for coins and now, new computers, swipe your credit card. Buy a house. I gather detritus from the street and hurriedly put them into the headless parking meters.

* *

Curbstones broken,
    Shattered asphalt,
Chopped into chunks by graphic assault.
I have a brass scale:
No matter how much weight
    I put on one tray,
It still never balances.
Frames lack pictures;
    Space depicts nothing.

The bare minimum,
    So invisible.

I've sucked on she-wolves' tits.

My brother and I cofounded Los Angeles.

Arma virumque cano.

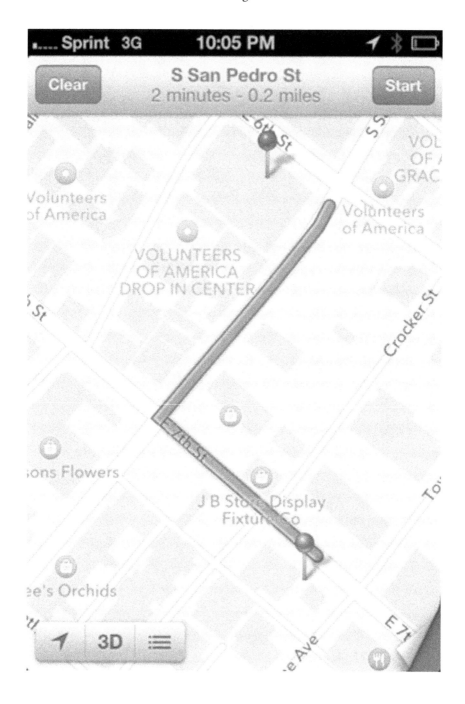

I wake up on San Pedro Street. In a doorway. On the walls are moths, plastered and smattered against the pale stucco, all dead. Attracted to the shining lights during the night. Deceased by daylight. Dead by morning. I have slept on the west side of the street. Looking east, towards the river, I see straight-line nooses to be, telephone wires north and south, and on the wires, perched, are 400 crows, perhaps more, all aligned like textbooks, like children in a row. One minute they are still; the next they flutter and fly—first a few of them, then the whole flock, one or two remaining, the noise like a firetruck, an emergency.

Crows are the smartest of birds. Corvids. They know more than I do.

Razor wire casts shadows,
Like witches,
Beneath the open window.

Ye Olde Taco House,

Tamales for the Danvers warlocks.

I am outside that window looking in,

Not inside looking out,

Intestines uncurled, unfurled,

Outside the carcass of the lamb.

* *

On Saturdays when I am clear, I walk up and down Broadway. I am in Mexico.

I hear voices in Spanish. I think I used to speak Spanish, but I am not sure.

An ice cream truck pulls to the curb by 5th Street. The driver turns on the musical lure. It is Beethoven's Für Elise.

* *

It all goes on forever.

Dust and shadows.

Endless understanding.

"Detritus in the crazy streets." Geoffrey Hill.
No, it's not leaves blowing, but it is a leaf blower.
I feel like undulating hills today. Today I feel like rocks.
Today I feel like orange peels.
Flashlights on and off,
Slick oil on the pavement.
Chatter in different tongues;
I boil glass.
Settled visions like coffee stains,
A dog digging at the dirt,
Paws pawing,
Chunks of earth giving way,
Shrugging dog shoulder,
Not finding what it's looking for,
Nonchalant: piss on the fire hydrant.
Wood bats, police batons,
      Broken broomsticks,

Animals that bore into the ground, birds pecking holes in trees.

The stains in the kitchen,

Torn towels on the floor.

I drink a can of beer,

Grab the shovel and start to dig.

Empty cages all around me.

Moths are stupid creatures—to fly towards light and death. Just like the rest of us.

I just write this shit down. That's all I have left.

* *

Circles of concrete,
Flashing lights;
Helicopters like paratroopers,
Or dragonflies,
Sidewalks scare me:
A sworn police officer,
The oath of office,
Promises kept and broken
Purple pills and red ones,
And bright yellow.
I swallow without water.
A pale blessing hangs,
Noose-like,
Over the burning city.

* *

Not knowing is knowing, and knowing is not knowing.
Information is not knowledge.

I saw a small blue thread on the carpet of the Barclay Hotel. I picked it up and put it in the trash. Then I thought that it might get thrown away. I had paid my twenty dollars for the night and I liked that little blue thread. So I took it out of the trash barrel and put it back on the floor. The trash barrel was beside my bed in the small room; it hadn't been emptied for days, nor for previous guests. But I couldn't bear the thought of that thread going to some dumpster. I looked at it back on the dirty carpet, in a slightly different locale from where it had been before. But it was equally vulnerable. It could get stuck to some one's shoe, mine even, and end up who knows where. I pick up the small blue thread. I put it my pocket.

"When they doused the folks on San Pedro, the cops braced me. Why me?" I wondered. They asked if I was imagining things…they inquired about my spectral evidence… "They were there," I said. "And they were dead."

The piece of thread will be indoors tonight & I will not. No. I picked it up. It's in my pocket.

Age not. Want not.
Who will be there to kiss me when they take me to the gallows?
We stood in line for food, holding hands.

* *

I'd only been out on the streets about a month. All's I had was a bedroll—no tent, no box, nothing to sleep in. I found doorways and alleys.
Then Albert started letting me sleep in his tent from time to time.
Sometimes she was there.

Messiaen at the Disney Concert Hall…

A few days after my security guard friend snuck me into the Disney Hall to hear Gillian Weir play Messiaen, I brought him a pizza. It took a while. These hipsters at Rocket Pizza ordered a large and couldn't come near to finishing their pie. As soon as they gave it to me, begging on 4th Street, Positively 4th Street, I ran it up to Jerome. I do not gauge embarrassment. But Jerome had a funny look on his face when I handed him the box. I don't think it was the greasy exterior. Gehry's building felt like aluminum foil in the toaster oven. Jerome scarfed down—that's a funny word, neckwear blowing in the wind—three slices of the pepperoni. I bid him farewell. I had to find G'Wayne, saving damsels on the street.

But first I stopped at the cathedral. A lesser architect. Moneo. But the Cardinal didn't think so…I'd rather hear the Mass in Latin. I stay the whole time…The organ plays brightly…I want to hear Messiaen and I shout out…the guards escort me from the church…I shouted three or four times I admit…Stained glass always seems to suggest Andalusia…iconography notwithstanding.

I should have kept a slice of pizza for myself. On the streets again, I am hungry now…if I shout here even the cops will pay me no mind….

* *

Perhaps "Miss Lonelyhearts" is the "Scarlet Letter" I wrote to my dissertation chair. Or maybe Tod Hackett is Hester Prynne.

You wonder sometimes even when you don't wonder anymore.

Doorway No. 1

Black, glossy stone. Two glass doors. Four-and-a-half feet wide. Knees bent. 5th Street.

Young Bekah

Hollywood and Vine: Bekah Before

My hands are shaking, but I am not on drugs. People have a hard time understanding that. I have a dog. I am often sitting or standing by the Hollywood and Vine subway station. I have a hat out. I am asking for money. When I am sitting, I am usually reading a book. I love to read.

"Go to rehab," one guy yelled at me.

I used to have a little apartment on Bronson Avenue, but I lost it when I lost my job. I came to Los Angeles from San Bernardino. Things were bad there. Things are worse here, but I can't go back now.

Yesterday, I was reading Poe. Today, I am reading Hawthorne's short stories. Yesterday, this one guy walks by. I've seen him before. He says, 'hi,' gives me a dollar most times. I think he parks his car at the Metro station.

Yesterday, he said, "good book," about my Poe volume. It's just a beat-up paperback. I got it at this used bookstore down the street. He was on his cell phone, so we didn't really talk.

I try and wear a little make-up. Sleeping outside takes its toll, but I think I am still a little pretty.

Today, the guy comes by again at about the same time. I am in the middle of a Hawthorne tale. This time, he stops to talk. He is not talking on his phone. "Poe yesterday, Hawthorne today. You've got good taste in books."

"I love to read," I say, then stop talking.

"I can see that." He fishes around in his wallet, looking for something to give me. "I see you out here," he says.

"I used to have a place…"

His phone rings. He takes it from his pocket and looks at the screen. "I gotta take this," he says. "Sorry."

While he is talking on his phone, he hands me a twenty.

"Are you sure?" I ask.

"Yes," he says and starts to walk away.

He looks over his shoulder and holds the phone for a second, "We'll talk another time."

I was just about to tell him what I thought of *Rappaccini's Daughter*. Instead, I stuff the twenty into my pocket, sit back down, and get ready to start reading "The Birthmark."

Rant

"You know why cop cars hit the gas?" He asked me.

"So they can go slow. Space so they never get there. It's black tar and green ice."

"I mean there are snakes and there are snakes, and then there's the Garden of Eden."

"You see the surface? Like it's wood or metal. I don't see that shit at all. I shattered glass. There's this guy on TV. I don't understand what he says. It's like he speaking Chinese, but he's not. I had a car. Now I don't have a car. I fucking walk. Use a fork; use a fucking knife. Who gives a shit? Right?"

"They sweep you away, that's what."

"Purple fans in the wind and we used to sit and like buy stuff in a red wagon, bruises and lights, and, like, fuck you man, fuck you."

He fell silent for a time, then he resumed.

"You got pebbles and you got rocks. It's not fucking personal, man. You know what I mean? It's like fucking lost fucking Atlantis, motherfucker I get all that shit. It's in the bag."

"Shards, you know what shards are? Asshole."

"Wine, beer. I just drink water. You believe me? Cocksucker!"

"We had a microwave in our house—like growing up they were invented by the Russians and the CIA; they wanted to kill us all. It's like microbes in microwaves. It's the same thing it'll fucking kill you. It mutates you. The way things, they toddle in. And eat you away. The KGB invented it. Them and the CIA.

"We run the place, comprende? It's the end of the line. But the night's not over. You know what I mean? You motherfucker. Comprende, you piece of shit. It is what it is, motherfucker. You don't know shit about what the fuck is going on, man.

"The sun is salty. It tastes like fish."

"It's all medicated minefields—we have a mushy mouth or she does or I do I'm not sure. But it's like Jolly Ranchers. It's up in the air. We had it all. You don't have shit, like you gonna talk to my ass? Fuck you. Times all around. It's like a circle."

The Neighbors Back Home

"Whatever happened to Lawrence?"

"Who?"

"You know, Helen's son."

"Oh, that boy. He moved to Los Angeles, didn't he? To go to school, I think."

"I seem to remember something like that."

"He was a good boy."

"Yes, that time when I broke my ankle, he would bring my newspaper up the driveway and right to my doorstep every morning on his way to school."

"Ms. Dell, his third grade teacher, still lives over right by the church. She still raves about him—as smart a kid as she ever taught and what not."

"Yes, physics, math—something like that."

"Not surprising that he was going off to some fancy school."

"Not at all."

"He was good to his mother, too, always helping her around the house."

"So sad when she took ill."

"Yes, not much more than a year after he left, wasn't it?"

"Surprising he's never come back to see her."

"Yes, at first he called her every day."

"I remember her saying that."

"Emily said she heard something bad happened to him."

"Really?"

"Murdered or something terrible like that."

"That would explain it, right?"

"Yes, it sure would."

"You know how dangerous they say it is out there in Los Angeles."

"Yes, I do."

"Depressing to see the house all empty now. The two of them seemed pretty happy."

"Yes."

"No other family that I know of."

"No, I don't think so either."

"Doesn't seem that either one of them will ever come back."

Dry Water

Clouds and winds increase my anxiety. My cardboard box cannot withstand rain. Drought scorches and parches, but I'm afraid of dark clouds. Birds on the phone lines crow louder than usual. On the streets, the dangers of water trump the dangers of dry.

Liturgy of the Word

The Mass Migration of the Homeless

They packed up their tents and their cardboard boxes and everything they owned, all now and all at once, and they began to move. They put their things in shopping carts and in backpacks and in anything else mobile and nothing else changed except they were on a march. The dirt brown smog still blocked the San Gabriel Mountains and there was of course still no way to see the sea.

"Who said for us to go?"

"It is time to go."

Later, no one could say where those voices came from.

Yet no one ceased to follow the sourceless command.

Dare is an awkward word, one destined to ambiguity and the ash heap. Doubt fares better. Nonetheless doubt in complete abeyance causes stirrings still.

At each step something was left behind: a shoe, a blanket, a memento mori, gravestones at Old Granary. Samuel Sewall is my hero.

From ashes to ashes, from dust to dust is no more than the Frst Law of Thermodynamics and vice versa.

But the shopping carts continue to roll.

The Army of the Ragged crosses Central Avenue and soon approaches Main, barricades at the gates, barbarians hard to find.

The trucks full of immigrants dispatched to gather back the stolen shopping carts meet resistance around Broadway and have no choice but to turn around.

The dreadlocked blonde girl is cuter than most. We stop along the route, pause along the pathway.

"What prompted this march?" I ask stiffly.

Through one bend of earshot and through the same refraction of the honeybee's eye, she says, "We must move on."

Another listen, ears bent 90 degrees, and she says, "I don't know."

Either way, the caravan approaches Main Street.

People are drinking Veuve Cliquot at Pete's Café. The widow watches warily. Time stops.

The LAPD intervenes.

But there is no time to go home, no turning back.

Godel is triumphant.

The parking meetings are full of remnants, stuffed with memorabilia.

Soon to be capped, the contents captured for all time.

The migrants do not get to Flower Street, let alone Figueroa. They magically turn up at MacArthur Park.

Shopping carts are unpacked, tents are reassembled.

Police presence vacates as the sun sets, officers off to greener pastures.

We de-camp.

Clara Bow dances at the Park Pavilion.

We fuck in the dark hotel. Nobody's paid the electric bill, nor for running water. Darkness is so romantic, candlelight hard to find. Moonlight is scarce. Her thighs are so pale they shine.

Nothing changes.

Little changes.

Everything changes.

The tent I pitch is not my own.

* *

Though not studied by Darwin to my knowledge, crows are said to be the smartest birds. I rarely fear the ravens that gather on the electric wires and perch on the telephone lines. O'Casey's crows steal hen-house eggs with impunity. Is it blue or rose, Picasso's "Woman with a Crow" of 1904? Or right in between? Crows crack open nuts using traffic, deploying signals—stop, go, walk, don't walk. This in Sendai, Japan. While across a thousand seas, Betty bends a wire. Not to mention New Caledonia.

Gleb returns home, to Dasha, but all is gone, all has changed, everything gone to shit. Livestock roam the streets, factories barren, most men dead, all life ravaged. I want to live in Pleasant Colony. I know what I am talking about, dammit!

Congratulations

Dear Lawrence:

Congratulations on your admission to the Graduate Studies program in American Literature. We are excited to welcome you to join our strong cadre of select students studying here at the University for a Ph.D.

Our world-renowned faculty will strive to support your scholarly efforts in order to ensure your success.....

Et cetera and so on....et cetera and so on....et cetera and so on....

Doorway No. 2

Green AstroTurf. Ten feet wide, one foot deep. Wet. San Pedro Street.

Lack and Loss

To include is not to condone.

Private thoughts are largely harmless; actions can be heinous.

Our common humanity is inclusively common.

We are all born of two people fucking in the night.

"Baby makes three."

Always alone, we are not alone.

Light is both particle and wave.

Stalin could be a loving father.

Herds are dangerous; groups are fundamental.

A hundred trillion bacteria live inside us. We are not individuals, but colonies.

The sociality of being.

Opinion is not judgment.

And vice versa.

Interpretation is necessary.

Doctrine is needless.

Collectivity is a requirement.

To ponder a coral reef.

Rights require responsibilities.

Freedom requires equality.

Not full egalitarianism.

But not merely equality of opportunity.

All concepts are conjugal.

We must revisit Hegel.

Observer-created reality may not be the whole truth, but it is a truth.

Reversing Dante's Circles of Hell, we must posit spheres of harm.

Gay marriage cannot hurt you.

If "it" hurts no one, then it is good.

The good old days never existed.

Salem, Massachusetts, 1692.

Montgomery, Alabama, 1953.

And on and on.

S & M and B & D are healthy; mob mentality is not.

Like E.O. Wilson, study ants.

For the good lessons and the bad.

NASCAR is scary.

Ultimate Fighting is scarier.

Guns do kill people.

Shoot the intolerant:

The best bumper sticker I can think of.

Augustine should have mitigated the swing of his pendulum; libertines have their place.

And their role.

Without the margins there can be no center.

Viva the margins!

Beware the righteous.

True believers pose the most danger.

Then the nihilists.

Punks are not nihilists.

No matter what they say.

Wall Street is nihilist, and shady: keep the profits; hand off the losses.

Robert Penn Warren: (We pass) "from the stink of the diaper to the stench of the shroud."

RPW (continued): "…out of history into history and the awful responsibility of Time."

Strategy precedes structure.

Blood is not thicker than water.

Garbage floats.

Judge not.

Judge sometimes.

Don't be afraid of clarity.

When wrong is wrong it is wrong.

Doubt, too, is a dear friend.

Original sin has nothing to do with sex.

Original sin is our boundless capacity to be cruel to one another.

Insomnia is the current universal condition.

Replacing, perhaps, Deleuze and Guattari's schizophrenic walking in the streets, which in turn replaced the person on the psychoanalytic couch.

I can't sleep.

Anguish.

I don't sleep.

Pride.

I never sleep.

In these times: invoke Beckett.

Or Shakespeare: Labor lost, no love.

To confuse means and ends.

To lose the larger end.

There is the text and so much more: thwarted longing, feeling maybe.

The tyranny of feeling: "I just felt like it."

The morality of feeling: to care.

Beautiful suffering necessitates the actions we never take.

Surrendering our larger public agency for a narrow small one—the newest gadget.

Power now is not diffused, but different, still central and concentrated—a big blanket smothering a multitude, or a suffocating gas choking millions, rather than a bat or baton breaking bones one at a time.

Steinbeck asked correctly: "Who do I shoot?"

Bloodbaths burst forth in South Bronx alleyways, not in boardrooms.

Contemporary anger is grossly misplaced.

Ditto our current attention to things.

And our love.

Anger is essential and necessary.

We speak.

Language mediates, allegedly.

Wars of words.

Echolocation.

Ants on stilts.

Taxonomy: Animals, Mammals, Primates, Humans.

Agency seen as action.

Iran, 1979.

Carter does nothing. Rightly.

The notion of zero.
Zero as invention.
In Arabia, as it turns out.
Nothing is the right thing to do.
At times.
Un-agency, non-agency, agency fully realized, unanticipated.
God is not dead, just grossly misinterpreted.

* *

The Rainy Season

My nose is wet like a dog's.

I have a cold I cannot shake.

Maybe it's more than a cold. I don't have a doctor to tell me.

On my good days, I can find a place to sleep—a zone of comfort, a refuge, away from the cold and the rain.

On a bad day, I rest, I slumber—in fits and starts—under the protection of cardboard, of wood pulp—sopping, soaking, leaking, wet.

* *

Our lives are not a matter of time but rather a product of duration. Time does not exist. Duration is how long we last. The age of electronics is the longevity of the battery. The longevity of the battery is the next outrageous fortune.

Networks span.

Julie Meheratu. Mark Bradford. I gather at galleries. Until I am asked to leave. I do.

Annoyed in a doorway, I try to sleep.

I have spent my pennies, my nickel and dimed.

I stay in doorways until I am moved on.

They ask me to move. I ignore them. They do not agree.

I dream. I unload instruments, mostly guitars, from the van. A bearded man threatens me. I smash his face. I bring out more guitars. This does not happen.

I think again.

Gustave Courbet: I write my manifesto.

I seek what I cannot find.

Doorways (In General)

A doorway is a dead-end, always closed, after hours, a place to sleep until roused at dawn;

Cracking skies, lineaments of clouds—sunrise, my enemy.

Sidewalks smashed with spoiled fruit, hydrants spurting water twenty feet into heavy air, Vagabond Man.

Shredded tires and empty beer cans. Dead dogs and live cats. The bleak river floats.

Fragmented garbage, mottled sunshine, molten wind.

Time has been unkind, cruel, unforgiving. Can time be anything? Can time be time itself?

* *

I suck at knowing what I want. That's because there is no yesterday.

I see Bekah in the lunch line at the Mission. I join her. Everybody gets mad at me.

"Hey, no cutting!"

"I'm with her."

"Get to the back of the line, fuckhead!"

Another person yells.

I cease to know who they are talking to.
I stand still.

They shout more.

I look to the sky. Swifts vault ten at a time down the chimneys of old buildings. A sign says "Bendix." The birds look like clouds.

I feel like a cloud; I feel like a bird.

A can hits me on the head.

"Get out of the fucking line!"

My ears ring and I cannot hear any more words.

A fight begins.

I reach for Bekah.

Police arrive.

They separate us.

Night arrives, and we are not together.

The cell fills.

I chew my skin.

They gamble.

Jail closes down.

No Bekah.

No light.

Salve Regina

There are cigarette butts and there are french fries, and empty potato chip bags, and crushed Coke cans, and plastic bags and paper bags, and when the wind blows, the trash and the detritus moves in Brownian motion, and when the day is still, it does not. And it is like a lab and it is not, and it is about the fate of the planet, and it is not. But it is just 5th Street and San Julian, and —as always—physics comes to bear. But my life is empty of order and of law. The police come and go, and sometimes they want to talk to me, and every so often it's an interrogation. And, it's always about the church. The one that exploded. Right away, we talked in the pews, or what was left of them...the cops and me. There was the sense that I had something to trade. If I could only say that Albert, or another man from the tents or the boxes, had sold drugs or that our neighborhood—our row—was infested with criminals, then the whole thing might go away...like a lost dog that you just forget about, though you never do...I could only pray: "Salve Regina, mater misericordiae, vita, dulcedo, et spes nostra, salve." Madonna by Raphael. But tell me. If I blew up the church, they said, then Albert was likely not guilty; and somehow, vice versa. Which makes no sense. Because neither was true, is true. I only went to the bathroom. In the back of the church, behind the cry room. I was simply absent. No more. Trading accusations. I know that is what they want; they are the Putnam girls. I was terrified at the explosion, but in my state of mind, and I still do know my state of mind, I ask—news accounts aside—was there an explosion? I have seen the RAF film; I know Carlos, and the Day of the Jackal... I pray silently now.

Dear Professor,

We have much to debate now about the origins of Modernity. Truth claims often cite the Fall of Andalusia, the "Discovery of America," the French Revolution.

But we also entertain arguments for the Renaissance, the Inquisition, the rule of Gregory the Great.

I understand the case for Gregory and the later manifestations of the Inquisition. Modernity needs bureaucracy and the ability to capture data and to store and document said data and the internal organization of enforcement. Stipulated.

My argument for the Salem Witch Trials as the starting point of Modernity persist nonetheless. As does my case for Los Angeles as the first After-Modern city, as per West's "The Day of the Locust."

It cannot be the case that Modernity begins before the onset of religious fundamentalism, allegiance to faith notwithstanding. The Ayatollah is little different from Bradford or Winthrop. The City Upon a Hill exists in many places. Continents run far and wide.

To argue differently puts us back to 3500 BCE, the invention of writing, the written form.

Surely we don't want to argue the pre-Ancients as Moderns.

I speak daily with Judge Hathorne, forebear of Nathaniel Hawthorne, Cotton Mather, and spectral evidence and the Putnam girls et al.

Space

I have no space, only doorways. Doorways defined. The space in front of a building. A boundary; a frontier; the space and place between. Cross-over. The River Styx. I cross over each and every night. Evicted; thrown out; asked to leave; cleaned out.

Doorways narrow and wet, sheltered and exposed; those who shout at me, those who speak softly, those who carry a big stick.

I am hurt but not stopped. I see trash and detritus, everything discarded— cigarette butts and beer cans, plastic bags and Styrofoam cups, all the things we do not need.

The sidewalk squares and asphalt patches; ladies push their shopping carts, sirens scream the noises of the night; I cannot sleep. I put everything I own in all the space I have.

It would be nice to see vistas, to look from off a hill. Crushed Coke cans obscure my path. I wash my hands. Sidewalks crack. Asphalt opens wide. The building's stucco is stained; I am in need of a bath. The road widens. I go nowhere.

It's free at the museum tonight and, despite my appearance, I go. Clearly it's not my crowd. I smell my armpits: not so bad. Still that girl looks at me. I look at my swollen feet. It's just the ankles really. Her ankles are fat too but it's different. She moves away. She has nice feet. My mother has nice feet.

Inside the museum gallery, they've hung three Rothkos. Red absorbs orange; purple swallows blue. The pulse of the womb. The cathedral at twilight. Do they depict the sacred or the holy? Holy is blessed and sanctified by another; sacred claims us all.

Oppositional, they're on walls across from one another. Bekah and I are across from one another. We look at the gum ground into the sidewalk. Sacred is otherworldly, maybe even pagan. I am no pagan but I claim the sacred. I bless Bekah's toes when I kiss them one by one.

Sacred is sacrifice and Rothko jumped out a window. Sacred is healthy and I am not. I do not like windows. Never have; never will.

All animals bite—not always but all too often. A dog follows me to my cardboard home. I ask it to go away—plaintively. I up my aggression. "Go away!" I shout. The dog was nice; now it snarls. I cannot go another night without sleep. I am not Kierkegaard. I used to make snowballs. I break bottles and surround my box with broken glass like a moat. My maps have been stolen and my books are torn and sundered.

The sun is broken today. I am glass today. I am a table. I am a parrot; I am a leaf. I am a window; I am wood. Once again, I cannot sleep.

Bekah's Mouth

Bekah is missing a tooth, but only just one. It's towards the back of her mouth—you can barely see it when she smiles.

When I kiss her, my tongue finds the hole in her mouth, and it stays there.

They serve spinach sometimes at the Midnight Mission, and romaine lettuce at Union Rescue—whatever it is, it sticks between your teeth.

Did Diomedes smile before he died? Did Diomedes die?

The story often comes back to my love for my mother.

Don't all stories return to the place they began?

White crosses watch the road to remember the dead. I can't drive any more, I can't see in the dark, I don't own a car, swollen sidewalks swallow my shoes, there's jazz in the alley, the lights are down low, I'm in love at the bar, cacti grow without water, her lips are so wet, the doorway is dry, I pack my bags eight times a day, the toy stores open at six, I fill up my cart, I hit the road, I shuffle two blocks, I look for Rebekah—my wheels just stop turning, the shopping cart has stopped moving, there are lines on the lot, the wheels have stopped turning, my lips are too dry, my belongings are damp, I move down the block, another big truck delivers its goods, the police, blue lights blare, Gregorian chants, pictures of nuns wearing habits, handouts rampant...

Books dis-shelved...I haven't shaved in weeks...Haven't had the chance.

Bekah has big lips. It's been four days. I miss her.

Parking Meters 1

They are replacing the parking meters on San Pedro. The brand new silver stems are staked in the ground, evenly spaced live gravestones at the Veteran's Cemetery. The meters are headless, open ends of cylinders, hollow dowels faced to the sky.

The stems are time capsules, hundreds of the silver scepters that need to be filled. I scoop up cigarette butts, soda tops, Frito wrappers and errant French fries, all manner of things discarded. I fill them up to the top. They'll get their heads back soon enough.

Interdiction

Between any two things, there is always a third.

Mediation is a third force, a broker.

Interdiction intercepts; it tries to break a chain.

Mediation claims no bias.

Referees, judges, binding arbitration.

Interdiction: power, seen and unseen.

One becomes the other.

The dialectic is displaced.

Dualism gives way to "plus one" or "minus one." "Among" displaces "between"

as the dominant preposition.

The introduction of the Trinity: A 3-way intervention.

The Father and the Son demand the Holy Ghost.

Then cyberspace.

The Trinity becomes the new minimum.

Quartet, quintet, sextet, ad infinitum...

Afterwards we have the problem of the tangent, of the intersecting line.

Amazing results.

Borders lose all meaning; frontiers retain meaning.

Hegel, Crick and Watson lose consciousness.

The ambulance leaves the scene.

Double turns triple.

I Need, I Want

Need a bath; need a shower; need a drink; need a fix; need clothes; need rocks and need stones; need time in Hawaii—maybe France; need the lowdown; need to hear my name; need Bishop to Queen-6; need to read about Fermat's Theorem; need to pull a daisy; need to meet a paleontologist; need roots; need a haircut; need to piss; need to sleep; want to visit a graveyard, to meet Hawthorne; want to see a doctor; want to watch television, to cheer, to see my mother, but I don't know if she's dead; I want to drink milk; I want a candle burning; I want Jack Sprat's fat; I want coffee—I want tea; I want you; I want me; I want a blue tie; I want to go home...

Dirtier

Inside her tent, we lit some candles.

When I rubbed the back of her neck, I could feel the grease and the sweat—weeks' worth of accumulation roiling under my fingertips.

Some of her nails were long and some were short. The cuticles were rimmed in black on the short ones; the long ones had grime caked under the length of them like dirt stuck on a shovel. She took my shirt off and her long nails scratched me. I could feel them part the rivulets of my sweat as she darted them along and around my shoulders, my back and my chest. I was very hard.

I took her hands in mine and I sucked her filthy fingers one by one, varying the pressure of my lips and tongue. She began to moan softly. I unbuttoned the top of her jeans and unzipped her.

She was very dirty and she smelled very strong and when I slipped her pants off she smelled even stronger. I pulled off her shoes; she wasn't wearing any socks. Her feet were filthy, too, of course, and the smell of her feet mingled with the smell of her pussy and her ass in the candlelit box we were fucking in. I began sucking on her toes, then licked up her calves, and back down to her feet. By the time I let my tongue linger along her thighs, then went down on her for good, she was dripping wet.

Broke

Busted broke,
The stuff of which nothing is made,
The grease at the bottom of the brown paper bag:
The whole world is mine.

Bekah wears jeans; Bekah wears corduroy; Bekah eats the baked potato.

E132—the cubicle at Public Storage that I once rented, when I had 80 bucks a month, a place for my books, my memories, a place for Bekah and me to sleep, to fuck, chased by guards and flickering lights, outsmarting said guards, doors open in our "unit," a bottle of Gallo Port...making out under the fluorescent lights turned off promptly at 9 PM.

Then and next: next and then: unable to pay, no eighty dollars, the stuff I brought now the stuff I lost...notice of auction, contents of Unit E132 for sale. Unpaid storage fee. Contents forfeited by owner. Sale to take place November 22.

No place.

Before the SRO

I never learned how to fix a car, or hammer a nail, or do anything with my hands. It's not that I never tried. My father said it mattered and, for a time, he was right. I might have made a living then. But that was before. Now if I could swing a hammer, I still wouldn't work. I cannot work. There is no work. Labor, no love. Love lost, labor lost. Love lost, no labor. Whatever. Gypsum mines and train lines. Steel towns and MoTown, making cars and money. Mills and manufacturing. That's been all over for a long time now.

It wouldn't have mattered anyway. It's not me. I could never change a light bulb.

Bekah walks the streets, but not that way.

I haven't been to my room at at the Roslyn Hotel for months. I hate being outside for so long. I still have blue thread in my pants pockets. I want my threads to be warm and safe. I have responsibilities.

I try to find my SRO friends, but to no avail. No pawn shops, no lingonberries, no long nails. All gone.

I still have friends.

Kings

Trash bags urinate rancid oil into vacant gutters, vibrant with remnants of fallen empires, Plantagenet kings deposed, redundant to the state of nature, sperm whale sputum—phlegm worth a fortune, everything monetized, washed up with seaweed on Aussie beaches, regurgitated or defecated into the Subaru hatchback of Loralee and Leon Wright, lucky unlike me.

The galley ship is the last to cross the line.

Midnight Mission mess hall dishes meals to Bekah and me. We stand upright at Runnymede, proud and still. A white Honda rounds the corner and skids into an oversized mailbox. Nothing happens; nothing ever does. Soiled gloves, boxing gym dismantled, grass overgrown.

Concrete crack, cactus spears; Bekah trips. I break her fall, unknown embrace, Garden of Eden, we take our meal side-by-side, as day retreats, my mind uncoils, the garden hose awry.

Jackets and Birds

A guy gives me a coat, a jacket really, and there is stuff in the pocket—old receipts and a napkin with a phone number, and some flecks of tobacco, an empty packet of gum, a book of matches with only two matches left, no advertisement; a broken pencil, unsharpened; the business card of a restaurant manager, a valet parking stub. The jacket is nice, navy blue, but a button is missing. I am really anxious because I want to throw away the contents of the man's pockets, but I cannot. I want to put my own things in the coat, my lucky quarter, I'm not sure what else, but something, something of mine, but I cannot. I cannot bring myself to do anything at all.

Pigeons come by to where I am sitting. I don't know why. I do not have food, and the man did not leave food in his pockets. I checked. One of the receipts says he ate at a place called Palermo's, an Italian restaurant, of course, because Palermo is the capital of Sicily, we all know that, and I don't think the jacket smells like pizza or garlic or anything. There is however bird-shit on the bench and the birds keep arriving. Added to the pigeons are sparrows and starlings. At my last apartment, I had crows, ravens, whatever you want to call them— Corvids, in any case, the smartest animals on the planet.

I like hotels. I have stayed in one or two of them before. Before is an important word to me because there is always a before and before was pretty. Except one day there was no yesterday. I understand that. But right now there was a before. For some people before sucks. For me, before had its advantages. I had things, for one.

I like birds, but I don't like these birds. I did not ask them to come here.

Pigeons are stupid, dirty birds.

Before, in the past, the crows on my clothesline could recite Shakespeare and "The Rime of the Ancient Mariner;" they could quote Milton and comprehend Anne Bradstreet. I adore ornithology.

I could give this coat away, but I will not. The pockets contain no nuts nor popcorn for the birds. I do not wish to feed the birds. And, I am not cold. I do not need a jacket, not tonight. Is there a "not now, not ever?" I am not Nietzsche. Nor Viggo Mortensen. I'm not the Lord of the Rings. Not ecce homo, nor homo faber. German movies are better than most, I admit!

I want to eat at that Palermo restaurant, but I cannot. I cannot afford to eat there. Before, I could. At one time, anyway. Sometimes I eat cold pizza now. When someone hands me a box of the slices of pizza they couldn't eat, couldn't finish. I always finish.

I feel small now. Sometimes I get this way, but not always. Before I did not, did not ever. Now I do. Not before. But maybe today is different. Maybe today it is just because the coat, the jacket the man gave to me, is too big, too big for me. The sleeves are long and the shoulders large and I could button Bekah in here with me if I could find her. I like the coat, the jacket, but it is definitely too big for me.

Becoming

Nearly everything can become anything else—lead to gold, a neutron into a proton, yes, almost anything. But not a quark into a lepton, or vice versa. Nor me into you, nor you into me, nor Thermopylae nor the Big Blue Bus into a limo, nor my tent on San Julian into a hillside home. But a caterpillar does become a butterfly and energy becomes matter, and vice versa. And sand becomes glass, and trees become rocks, and Pompeii becomes lava, and coasts become oceans, and rain becomes ice, and monuments become rubble, and tyrants live forever, and Lincoln's DNA becomes mine, and mine becomes his, and the begotten become begotten, and my diner becomes a bistro, and the storefront becomes abandoned and then becomes revived, and pornography becomes sex, and lives become lifeless, and plants become putrid, and the dead come alive, and the tires go flat, and the jobs go overseas, and the carbon dioxide ascends, and the Virgin ascends, and the Assumption begins, and the Resurrection subsides, then waxes and wanes, and as the banal leaves turn colors, and the police flash their badges, and skyscrapers rise and then fall, and the soup lines form, as the interrogation begins, and the power lines fall, and my blanket tears and my food rots and my Bekah is gone, and my life never changes.

Starched shirts and high cheekbones and Indian jewelry and a vest and torn tee shirts and I am lonely.

Ever not always.

Analysis

At first you have nothing.

So you just lay down in a doorway. You just find a place to sleep. A place with some room.

Then you get smart about it. You find cardboard, a large box. Somehow refrigerator boxes abound. Fortunately.

Then you move up.

Wallet

"Give me your wallet!"
"Wallet?"
He slaps me.
I haven't had a wallet in years.
"I don't understand the question," I say.
He hits me again.
I don't react.
He repeats the question, or rather his demand.
Bekah laughs.
The guy walks away.

Sieve

Sieve is a word that has a lack—a lacuna and a hole, a blockage and a strain.

Fish stumble on the pathway, ill-suited;

She trips on trash in the alley —

A cut on the sole of her foot—I fix it.

Sounds seeming unperturbed,

Trucks deliver templates of things to come,

Birds are missing feathers:

The police arrive like Henry at Agincourt.

Be gone with us!!

Daily

Stains stain my blanket and I fold it over the fold, and it is night, so I spread it over my body, the whole of it, and it comes up short whether wet or dry, and I memorize—or rather just look at—the pattern and the color, and it is red and it is rust and the shapes are not flowers. Nonetheless I am neither cold nor hot, and the distilled lights before morning, all in the gray and the blue, an odd light, neither dark nor light, neither day nor night.

Inside my box, I fold the greasy wrappers in half, and then I smooth them out in full and in toto, making layers like sediment—Carl's on top of McDonald's, Taco Bell on top of Burger King, KFC before Del Taco—the onslaught of history: Hammurabi, hieroglyphics, Hittites; the Rent Boys have vacated the premises.

Pigeons peck in the morning.

Litter stirs in the wind.

Fold and fold again.

Pack and push on.

Dissertation

Dear Professor Martin:

Despite Dada and the theater of the Absurd—if you don't give me "Locust"—you have to give me "Lonelyhearts" and "L'Etranger." Despite writing "historically," Hawthorne was still a contemporary of Balzac, and a predecessor of Crane's fallen women, especially Maggie. There's materiality there, in all of it—and, at the same time, the ghost of "spectral evidence." People of the Book, I beseech thee! The Jeremiad arrived in Los Angeles, the fallen Mecca of destroyed and destructed dreams. It came in the trunk of the car of Nathan Weinstein—the depressed John Winthrop of the West.

We all agree the Protestant work ethic transmogrifies into hyper-consumerism.

Two hundred and fifty years of the hollowing out of the American soul brings us from Hester Prynne to Faye Greener.

The Book of Revelation revealed: "the depiction of portents, unnatural or extraordinary occurrences, read as signs; a sense of irreversible deterioration if values and behavior, incapable of correction by purposeful reform; a centerpiece catastrophe, imminent or actual, which will radically alter the status quo frame of reality; and accompanying final judgment; and, the coming of a new world, frame of reality, or consciousness to replace what we destroyed." (Lewis, op. cit.)

We know what's coming.

Savonarola and Torquemada die in the same year, as do Shakespeare and Cervantes.

Faye is not Hester, but rather what Hester has become—defiled by what the Puritans always were, forever had been, omnia secula seculorum—minus all pretense, valid or invalid, legitimate or not—a woman in Los Angeles now in the pulpit of Wilson and Dimmesdale: "Come, come to me," she rides a motorcycle up the isles between the pews....Tod Hackett whisked away in a police car and a stabbing on Black Friday at a Wal-Mart over the mass-produced scarcity to be found on their shelves.

All the Noises of a House I Do Not Hear

Creaking wood

Groaning pipes

Leaves blown

Bushes clipped

Dogs barking

Sidewalks jack hammered

Children crying

Ice cream trucks singing

Trees swaying

Water running

Kettles whistling

Vacuums running

Alarm clocks beeping

Heaters hissing

Pans sizzling

Beggar

It's a beggar. He, she, or it. Pronouns. Famished. Starving. Which is the comparative, which is the superlative? I have to ask to eat. No, I have to ask others in order to eat.

At the corner of 6th and San Pedro, I watch a crazy man feed pigeons with popcorn. He wears no shirt, though it is February and by no means hot. I scoop or scoff or scarf a handful of the popped corn before the pigeons flutter and land, fighting and pecking one another as they clack and claw on the potholed pavement.

Bekah ate last night. We were not together. I wish we were. But not for the food.

They broke the cardboard boxes and they smashed our tents and they repossessed our shopping carts and they returned them, empty, to Ralphs and all the other markets, and we had nothing left and no neighbors anymore because our stuff and our place was gone.

And they arrested Albert and they detained Joey and they rousted Annie and they arrested Big Dog and they took Phil the Dentist to the hospital and they arrested Fat Johnny and they arrested Bonds and they arrested Billy and they arrested Alfie and they arrested Lisa and James and Paul and Matthew and Luke and John.

And then most of us were gone.

I had a dollar in my pocket, and with all the dismay and disruption, I entered the 7-11 and purchased, bought, transacted a bag of Fritos.

The chips tasted delicious. Salt and light. Loaves and fishes. Churning days, searing nights.

Dumpster

They take out the trash on Tuesday

They empty the dumpsters on Thursdays

The streetlights sometimes flicker

Very few Popes ever resign

Canons scatter shrapnel

Claiming the blood of the guilty

Tulip bulbs ache from time to time —

Frozen fields in Flanders

Flemish painters make their mark

Operation Clean Sweep

On the streets of Downtown Los Angeles

Withered weeds grow beneath the trash bin's footprint

Neither one of us has eaten for days

Scarcity - worship the current cult

Riven river overflown —

Dry skin, cracked knuckles, sodden matches

Spokesperson for the District Attorney

Speaks to the crime on the 11 o'clock news

Tweet what you've seen:

Car chase, beggar-man, loitering, littering,

Spitting on the sidewalk, dandelion nutrients,

The erupting asphalt roars

Tree roots rip concrete slabs uprooting sidewalks —

I scarcely move

I barely flinch,

Aware the era has ended,

The epoch over,

Groceries go un-bagged, empty shelves—

Peter the Venerable grants posthumous absolution to Abelard

At Heloise's request

Of course the Cistercians hated the Cluniacs —

Rousted early, rousted late,

It's time to move on, to move, to go on;

I don't want to move,

I have no intention of doing so,

I defy your order to order me to go

I gather my belongings,

I pack up my things

I risk excommunication,

I refuse to kneel in the snow —

Paved parking lots reign over the last of the Plantagenet kings —

I refuse my place in line.

Another Bekah

It didn't seem so long...the time between things... The smell of my mother's feet, my dissertation, Bekah...It's all unclear...we have no fucking idea...not about nothing, not about shit...I spend my time studying bivalves...scallops, clams and mussels...can you crawl?

My crows on my telephone wire, my tumbleweed connection, beside the tent that I do not own, my neighbor Albert, my Plantangenet king—sovereignty!— my Bekah, biblical girl...

You are not the wife of Isaac nor the mother of Jacob and Essau; you are mine, standing alone in line at the Midnight Mission...it is not the end of days, but rather our beginning, you and me...perhaps you are mine!

Help me, Hester, help me!

Dude, you have an Ahab beard!

Skater punk wino, sheer walls falling...

I love the girl standing in line...her name is Rebekah...

She told me she grew up in Boston and New Hampshire…live free or die... granite, sandstone, limestone, shale...igneous rocks and other rocks...Bekah is taller than I am...I am Tod Hackett in love... Burn, baby, burn!

"I was chillin' at 64th and Crenshaw when Reginald Denny got his ass kicked...I drove out and we watched the rest on TV...I don't have a TV..."

Is there a concept behind Los Angeles burning? Or does something just burn?

A city? A place? A structure? A monk?

But Bekah...biblical daughter, biblical mother, biblical wife...My girl...

I hold her hand in line at the Mission...We wait for sermons and soup.

I tell her I love her nose ring; I truly admire it; my mother had her nose pierced.

"Indeed he will be blessed."

"Do you love me, Bekah?"

I understand that I have sold my birthright...you cannot fool me...

The curtain burns and the dwarves rule the streets...certainty collapses amidst uncertainty; confusion rules confusion...I take Bekah's hand...not in marriage but in truth...I abhor analytic philosophy...let me count the ways in which Wittgenstein was wrong...

Bekah, I love you—not in language...but in deed, indeed, indeed...this is when. And where I cannot think...

Bekah, please hold my hand...

My library books are overdue…this means a lot to me...to have no fines..."forgive us our debts as we forgive our debtors..."

She knows, I think...Bekah knows...I have this lucky quarter...A 25 cent piece.... my mother gave it to me...she gave it to me right after she slapped me. I didn't need a reward...I loved it when my mother slapped me...I really did...it felt so good...no bullshit...Bekah is always gentle, except when she is angry...I don't mind when she is angry...her feet are both smooth and hard...

Remember when the guy in Grapes of Wrath says "who do I shoot?" I am that guy.

When I rub Bekah's dirty feet, I think of my mother. Maybe mom lives in Ohio, or maybe Massachusetts where I grew up, but I remember the smell of her feet. I loved that smell that the rest of the family hated…I always wanted my mother to take her shoes off when no one else did…the smell of her feet repelled my father and my siblings, but not me.

Bekah has those feet!

Oh, yeah, my lucky quarter:

My other gave it to me—oh, shit, my mother, not my other…I took out the trash or something, something that brought me favor…

Whatever, she gave me this quarter, to keep or to spend, and I put it in my pocket, this George Washington and eagle coin, and I slipped it into that little stopwatch, pocket watch kind of place, and I kept it there…And it stayed there… And when it was there, it made me worry, like I always thought I would lose it…

"Neither ashes nor soot…"

That Quarter made my palms sweat…but I had it in my grasp, my clutches…in omnia saecula secaelarorum."

From pants to backpacks to pockets…in my shirt, in my hat…Washington, eagle, drummer boy, emblem, stateside…I DO NOT LOSE THINGS !!!

When I dropped it under the table at the food hall at The Mission, my Bekah found it for me.

Thought

We are all thought. Thoughts are just numbers. There are only two numbers: either/or; both/and. Thoughts are all we are; thoughts are all we are.

Public thoughts, private thoughts. Which is squashed like an ant underfoot?

Bottle in Hand

Money in my hand and a bottle, I sit on a park bench.

I do not feed the pigeons.

I want someone to sit beside me.

I look again in my pocket and in my backpack. My lucky quarter is still not there.

My mother used to tell me "it will turn up."

I keep hoping, and look. But it's been two weeks now.

Lead us not to evil.

Bottle in Hand 2

Money in my hand and a bottle, I sit on a park bench.

I do not feed the pigeons.

I want someone to sit beside me.

I look again in my pocket and in my backpack. My lucky quarter is still not there.

My mother used to tell me "it will turn up."

I keep hoping, and look. But it's been two weeks now.

Lead us not to evil.

A man arrives with popcorn. He feeds the pigeons. They flock close and around, flapping wings. I do not flinch but I want to. I remember a professor of mine, and his love for Darwin's Finches. (Tanagers, actually.)
The bird-feeding man is gone. I am alone again on the bench. No one nearby.

Bystanders: Bekah Again

Crumpled wire, crumbled steel, broken brick—bystanders;

Skies unshaved.

Dirty clothes chafe undesired.

We huddle around the burning trash.

We kiss.

Your cheap trashed camera points much too close to my face;

Yet it takes no pictures; it records nothing at all.

Nonetheless I love the movement of your scrawny finger as you snap the imaginary images.

Don't worry: my memory has not failed me. There is no such thing as failure as long as I am alive.

The fire wanes. We seek warmth.

You throw plastic bags on top of the fleeting embers—Cheetos bags melting quickly, hovering like cumulus clouds or a toxic fog, above the scraps of busted furniture, heaps of discarded detritus, lost, thrown away, unwanted—like severed limbs.

Our prosthetics are unavailable,

So we hold each other tight in the darkened cold,

All else extinguished.

Bulldozers

The needles and the bottles, and the broken glass and the syringes and the cigarette butts, and the shattered glass and the used needles, and the condoms, and the dead rodents, and the dirt and the cellophane, and the broken things, and the miscellany and the needles and the condoms, the packing material, and the tape, and the cellophane and the Cheetos bags, and the apple cores, and the crushed French fries, and the mush, and the aluminum foil, and the mud, and the emptied packages of Sudafed, and the broken pipe, and the needles and the condoms, and the broken park bench and the shattered sidewalk and the dead trees, and the needles and the cigarette butts and the condoms - - oh, the blessed meadow.

Referrals

"Go to Midnight Mission, they will feed you."

"Go to Skid Row Housing, they will give you shelter."

"Go to the Department of Social Services, they will find you health care."

"Go to DMH, they will find you a counselor."

What is DMH?

"Go to the Department of Agriculture, they will get you food stamps."

"Go to the SSA, they will get you SSI."

"Go to LAUSD, they will help you get a GED."

I have a Master's degree.

Street:

(prior to the first session is the title "Official")

"Get a job."

"Fuck off, you freak."

"Eeww."

No response.

No response at all.

No response whatsoever.

"Fucking bum!"

No response.

Policy:

"I don't see why the government should be in the hand - out business."

"We can't afford these kinds of services in the current budgetary climate."

"Let them read the Want Ads."

"We need to show compassion in our State budget."

"We should give them a Smart Card and let them manage their own funds."

"We can build transitional housing with embedded medical services for pennies on the dollar."

Miscellaneous/Diagnoses:

ATM

COPD

ADHD

ADD

PTSD

AS

BD

BPD

CODTP

EDD

DPSS

HUD

HHS

Watch

"What time is it?"
They ask me on the street.
I stare at my bare wrist.
Do you know what time it is?
The clouds are complete today.
"Do you know what time it isn't?"
Black gum stains spot the sidewalk.

Abraham

I'm just like Abraham; or he's just like me. I mean we hear voices. God didn't tell Abraham to kill Isaac. Who would do such a thing? Abraham lost it for a while, was hallucinating, fucked up in the head. Just like me. God didn't tell him to pull out the knife; God talked him down from the tree. That's why you still have stories of Isaac. And that's why you had Jacob and Esau. I mean had Abraham done the deed, end of story.

Bottom Feeders

I am exhausting my knowledge of geology, of science.

I know little about rocks; I do not know the names of trees.

Evergreen vs. deciduous. That is it.

I prefer that leaves fall off and die.

Systellapsis debilis spend daylight hours in the Mesopelagic Zone. By contrast, they swim very close to the surface at night.

Edward Forbes (1815-1854) believed deep oceans had no life.

He was wrong.

Bottom feeders confirm my birth, my life, my existence—I suck that sand. Pictures hang in the Holocene. I never piss my pants.

St. Louis: "At the time of the murder, Lee Shelton owned a nightclub called 'The Modern Horseshoe Club'…"

Physics

What's the shortest distance between two points?

A straight line.

What's the distance between truth and power?

The circumference of a circle.

Equation: C = Pi x D

Is power always bad?

No, of course not.

Power is work.

10th grade physics.

The DWP.

My electric bill.

Then they "move" us two streets over.

Off of Los Angeles Street.

To make way for the arts.

We have re-defined "the event."

I still search for Bekah amidst and among the headless parking meters.

* *

I am like Dark Matter; I am inert. I do not interact. I lurk. I walk San Pedro Street in silence.

On the bleeding sidewalk the broken glass remakes itself in the shape and shadow of a crow.

I read avidly of alienation in doctor school; now I am disconnected. I do not like it.

Then I was tall; now I am short.

My eyes were once green; now they are blue.

I have misplaced my French Horn.

The sounds of battle ensue.

My knees do not buckle.

When he raises his hand, I hit him.

Now I am in trouble.

* *

Inside jail there is space and no space.

I am geometry.

Or a limit approaching zero.

Half the distance to the goal line.

I have no goals.

Pilgrims

We obsess on the parts,

We count the components;

Circuit boards and microchips:

Our inventory is full of detail –

The number of slaves on the ship,

All the tea in China,

Billions of burgers sold.

Constantly, we misread the obituaries;

Consistently, we undercount –

Census workers at my doorstep.

Just a tiny indication.

Still I read Anne Bradstreet,

Whom I shunned in junior high,

Continually turning aside her poems,

Unworthy of my attention.

Now I print her portrait from her entry on Wikipedia,

I long for her,

Her tercentenary long past,

Her 400th anniversary still to come.

My classics teacher wore her skirts short,

And her nails were very long –

Just a hint of things to come.

"That we live no more, we may live ever."

Entropy notwithstanding,

It is the whole that counts.

For all the whiskey in Ireland;

For what do I sell my soul?

For the world over, I say,

For the world again, all over,

For my teacher's sexy clothes.

* *

We're at the corner tavern.

The lights are out;

Perhaps they were never on.

No big, no bang.

She scratches my face;

That is how I know who it is.

I begin to bleed;

She does it again.

I know the history of blood,

Plantagenet and Tudor,

The Czar notwithstanding:

"Should we stay?"

"It's your call."

I forget who's speaking,

Whose, who —- hoot, hoot…a screech!

Voices trail off;

Owls are not ravens,

We have evermore.

Suddenly the lights go on and off,

This time for sure;

They remain liminal, in hyper-position,

Both particle and wave.

You scratch me again;

Again I bleed.

Science bears down.

"We should go," you say.

I hesitate.

"It is not a question."

I reach for my drink.

"Leave it on the bar!"

The music is way loud,

We walk out the door;

I remember the number ten.

Rain

I stay at the bar because I know it will rain.

Our SSI checks are spent and gone.

I have a cane I do not use.

It begins to rain.

If we had sun I would be wealthy, wondering if—not how—the world works.

First rain: I do not know where to go, what to do.

If I had a phone and she had a phone, I would call Bekah—but we do not.

Cardboard does not repel rain. Centuries do not end. Two more bucks buys another beer.

Squished

Squished and squashed inside the van, I hope they don't hate us, hate me.

I'm looking for that girl coming from Sonora, but it seems that the police are here.

I know it's not my Bekah, but I don't know who it is.

Packing like tuna, shipped from Monterey, canned in Stockton, Teamsters Union, Huelga, El Pueblo Unido, the 5 to the 99, up and over the Grapevine, past Magic Mountain, the van full, water at nozzles, turn your AC off, if you have it at all, overcrowded, cargo van, mini-van, no hybrids, no Mendel, pea plants excluded from the experiment—tall plants, short plants, pea pods—watch the van, empty now, no Bekah…..

Friend's Story

Lingonberries/Post Doc

We were watching the news on 27 channels at the Sears (and Roebucks) in Glendale, California.

It was cloudy but not raining.

We counted the televisions. There were exactly 27—maybe 28 if we missed one. But I don't think so. In any case, it would always be higher, never lower.

At nearly noon, or maybe exactly at twelve, somebody started changing all the channels.

Then we—just the two of us—began to change the channels, too. We had whales and football and "I Love Lucy" and all on different stations.

Security got wind of all this.

We got caught.

They did not.

Security asked us to leave.

We exited the store without argument.

Cluny was all holy but intolerant. Better in the end, outcomes aside, to be Abelard.

We drove the car away from Glendale.

At Ikea in Burbank, we bounced between living rooms and bedrooms, bookcases and children's furniture, kitchens and bathrooms—our imaginations ran wild.

"I want to eat here," she said. "I love lingonberries."

"OK," I said. "That sounds cool."

We left the showrooms to disembark at the Ikea restaurant.

She ordered Swedish meatballs and we asked for extra lingonberries.

They gave us six containers of the Scandinavian fruit.

"Excuse me," she said, in the middle of our meal. "I have to go to the bathroom."

After she had been gone for ten or fifteen minutes, I started to wonder.
I thought about all kinds of things.
I randomly looked under my tray and I found a note.
"I've gotta go," the note said. "Thanks for the lingonberries."
I slept the whole night in our car.
I don't know where she spent the night.

History: The Pawn Shop

I took my girlfriend to the pawnshop to show her all the things we'd never have.

* *

I just got out of jail. I was having a hard time finding a job.

* *

At the dimlit bar, they were talking about Mesopotamia, but they were fucking it up. They had it all wrong. They didn't know shit about either the Tigris or the Euphrates, not to mention Nebuchadnezzar. Maybe they knew about Felujah or Abu Ghraib. But maybe not. And, even if they did, what did they know about the Sumerians or the Assyrians, or Ur or Uruk, or cuneiform writing, or the origins of written language, or the Epic of Gilgamesh, or history or pre-history, or the development of agriculture?

* *

I fall in love every ten minutes or so—mostly on the bus, the Metro, the Dash, the Big Blue Bus, the way those of us without money get around in Los Angeles.

I take the bus to look for a job.

I follow the girls that I fall in love with. I get off at their stop, which is never my stop.

I walk behind them on the street.

I never talk to them. That is not true. The never part. This one time I did.

I don't ever tell my girlfriend.

* *

We stole a car, but we got caught.

I went back to jail.

Though she was with me, my girlfriend got off. First offense. Six months' probation.

She wrote to me in jail. She said it was over. She was sick of our lives, sick of me, sick of my shit. She said that I would never change. She was right. I never wrote back.

* *

I got out of jail again, and she wasn't there, and she would never be there again.

That I knew for sure. Without a doubt.

I went straight to Skid Row, where I knew there were women who wanted me. I was right again.

Carla was sunburned and weathered and her skin was rough like a cowgirl's, over-exposed to the sun.

She bit her nails, but her fingers were long and beautiful, and I kissed them, and I kissed her all over, and I bought her drink after drink, and drinks for me, too, and we fell in love.

* *

We moved in just before they tore the building down.

The demolition crew came early in the morning, and we could hear the foreman barking orders.

We gathered up the few things we had, and we left to find another place to live.

I had nothing, really—except Carla—and I was as happy as I'd ever been, walking away, holding her hand as the building came down.

The Other Side of Light

Darkness is just the other side of light. For redemption to rule, perhaps it must get a little darker…

Dead animals—some domestic, some wild—lay across the road in droves. Renée Razer emerges from the red house.

* *

Renée has long red hair. I know her by name only.

* *

I don't want to know why the world exists, or how it works. Who cares? I want to know what the world is.

Diner

I ate at a restaurant for the first time in years: a diner without truck drivers, a mile from Union Station, a block from the cardboard box I call home.

The cool kids order, late night, the things that I don't. Negation is my circumstance. Detroit makes what I do not own. Certainly I am not cool. Detroit makes cars. A gaggle of tourists photograph I know not what. I like to read but I cannot buy books. Even when I can still read. Blue skies void me. I long for clouds.

Bekah's hair falls like water. I love her bitten nails. Her legs launch like train cars. My luggage parts my company. Bekah seems sideways. Silhouette, I am not sure if her breasts are large or small.

Time-capsule parking meters, headless horses. I had my say in the Rump Parliament; I fought in Oliver's Army; I register voters in MacArthur Park, watching the detectives, Bekah resplendent in vermillion and cut-off shorts, the apartments next door full of Haitian girls and citizens of Vietnam. Mea culpa, nyet.

Bekah is back and I found my quarter. It is a good day.

Elementary Particles

The lady gave me money. Dollar bills, not loose change.

All we are are thoughts. Thoughts are all we are. In fact, everything is a thought. There are no tables, no chairs, no fingers, no bones. That's why I live here.

Crass, crude, or sublime.

Base or elevated.

Undifferentiated. In my case, at least.

I am hungry. Who is God?

Human, non-human, and inhuman.

All a synapse.

Jaguars hunting, spiders spinning, tourists at the Disney Hall—looking, snapping pictures, missing the point.

Indistinct, indistinguishable. Only after thought, after-thought, is order possible. Then morality, and its opposites. Random order, order imposed, re-thought. Fundamental to foundational. Deconstruction, reconstruction, reconsideration.

She had no idea what I was talking about.

G'Wayne

G'Wayne proclaims the word, preaches every evening on our very own Wall Street: "Drought is our dream come true, the answer to our prayers. Crops fail to comfort us. Pray for pestilence. I must continue my search."

"Pater noster, qui es in caelis...fiat voluntas Tua, sicut in caelo, et in terra.."

My eye turns as I listen to G'Wayne. On the next corner west, a man dressed in red white and blue spins a sign to attract customers to a new chicken place.

"I came to bury the oil, not to drill it...the downpour did not come, be thankful, brothers and sisters...

"Thank God Almighty, we are not wet."

I take my lucky quarter out of my jacket pocket and I put it in my pants pocket, the one made especially for change, the one with nothing else in it.

"We are not people of the ship! Our numbers add up to more than twelve. I am writing to the Lottery Commission. I want you all to sing my petition! Praise God!"

Bekah listens in rapt attention.

As always, I take her hand.

**

G'Wayne wants me to come with him to the Lottery Commission. It's in the Reagan State Office Building.

I am not in good shape today.

I tell G'Wayne this.

"Aw, come'on, man," he says. "You gonna make me go by myself."

The woman at the desk is an apricot, and I am an egg. I tell her this.

G'Wayne mad-dogs me.

"And, you, my friend, are both a table and a chair. If we had toast...hey, how about breakfast?"

I put some shit from my pocket on her desk.

The lady picks up the phone.

G'Wayne yells at me, but I cannot hear what he says.

"Chastity in hallway so that do not run indoors...that do arrangement putting in order in place after infancy lotus width use...hospital schedule dimension close adhesion consultation...gauze that is biting must be biting certainly firmly 2 or 3 time...I am responsible for bleeding if surrender beforehand. Saliva swallows without spewing...Let's help to ability elevation... to speak announcement much and greatly lacteal gland...Good manners... do not handle seat that extract this with hand...I enlist Department after a week...I eat nicely..."

Peter Handke

It didn't seem so long....the time between things...The smell of my mother's feet, my dissertation, Bekah....It's all unclear....we have no fucking idea...not about nothing, not about shit...I spend my time studying bivalves...scallops, clams and mussels...can you crawl?

Lo and behold, there is a knock at my door. It is Peter Handke. I offer him Wild Irish Rose and he comes in. I ask him about the Serbs and the goalie; he does not respond to my specific requests. He talks mostly of his mother's suicide.

Parking Meters 2

Fourteen Buddhist monks kneel to pray in Pershing Square. They chant in protest. To what, I cannot tell. They kneel in formation: two in front, then four rows of three. We watch in amazement at the stillness.

Late at night, Joey and D'Wayne and Albert and Jorge and Bekah and me drape our blankets over some parking meters on San Julian. Under the streetlights, they look like the monks kneeling in prayer.

Misfit

Miss Fit becomes MisFit—strolling straying streets, stultifying—pursued by me, Lawrence—missing Bekah, lost again—unconsoled, inconsolable, walking Wall St., San Julian—boxes, tents, tents and boxes—pondering how to say desperate—rainy night, unwanted, thinking of another solution—untrod, unfucked, wishing mahogany—Bekah—broken shoelace outside the hardware store—barefoot—unbroken, un-rain, clear skies now—later rain again—I fled, she fled…

History: Café Vanille Bakery

I burn my fingers baking the expensive bread

That I cannot afford to feed to my own children,

Except for the stale loaves they let me take home.

Power

As dawn breaks in a shattering sunrise, windshields broken in scores of cars, parked idly, facing west, I am shushed from the jeweler's doorway, hosed down, big dogs barking, divine equality ever displaced by displacement; streetlights on automatic timers, controlled by computers, glow down in the sunrise, the emerging city—the policeman telling me the body thrown from a 3-story walk-up had splattered on the pavement like strawberry jelly spread on burned toast —- just last night—just outside the self-named Red Line, at the terminal of the corporately-named Union Station, a nation divided. I plead for Bekah, my White Whale, my security, my Anne Boleyn, my Mother of Jacob and Esau, and she is lost to me; I don't know where she is, but I know she will come back to me. This is what I know in the morning when the City comes to life.

* *

The specter of power over power recedes in newly anodyne Los Angeles; falsehoods prevail over falsehoods while the cops club Crazy Carl to certain death and I remember the crows gathered on the clothesline, the bits and bytes that constitute the universe, the multiverse, just outside my grasp, gumshoe streets soaked in a sudden rain dropped from the sky as mythology, as legend and lore, unremembered and unforgotten, the Pacific Siren breaking my bough, Operation Safe Streets sweeping my sidewalk, confiscating my property and my friends, annihilation in analogue form, no digitized content —- not now—the authors of authority in full action, my prayers unanswered, our village vanished, swept—as it were—under the rug of irresistible power, while the rain begins, at first softly, then with increasing pressure, the kind that makes your skin tighten,

I put an "L" and a "D" on the bridge.

I want to make my mark.

Tagger Kingdom!

"Dude!"

"What?"

"You're gonna get us arrested."

A car full of kids speeds away.

Cops arrive.

"What the fuck are you doing?" the big cop asks.

"I'm looking for Bekah."

"What?"

The other cop pats me down.

"He doesn't have shit."

No spray cans, no Sharpies.

Near the bottom of the blue picture of the magenta Madonna I place my initials—LD—in oil. Faint traces of my tag remain after white wash occurs.

LD splayed and splashed all around town.

Billboard life: spread mobile ion bus routes, train stops, Bakersfield Station—half-hour delay. Grape, orange, brick, unreinforced concrete, fame and ruin.

Cic LA Via

The vegan bicyclists beat me silly. They are a violent lot. They hit me with hand pumps and wrenches, clubbed me with water bottles and with their fists. I was packing up the only tent I'd ever owned. Clearly, Los Angeles is going downhill, spinning out of control.

History: Starkness

I step inside the King Eddie.

I am thirsty from my time in the desert and from the drive.

I order Irish whiskey and soda.

A woman with broken teeth sits down beside me and we begin to talk.

Her face is weathered, but her hands are oddly smooth and her skin taut and almost delicate.

I buy her a whiskey, and then, a little later, I buy both of us another round.

After a while, I step outside to the corner to smoke a cigarette.

The guy watching my car flashes me a thumbs-up sign and I return the gesture.

I stare east down 5th Street. The city appears dark and dirty as my sightline telescopes towards Alameda.

Stark.

I flick the cigarette butt into the gutter and head back inside for another drink.

The woman with the smooth hands has her bare feet up on my barstool. She smiles at me with closed lips.

In a stark world death would come by thirst or by violence.

I have only alcohol and nicotine to end my day.

For now, she has me.

It is the right ending to one of my ever-desolate days.

Tent

Putting up a tent is faster than taking it down. That's what Albert told me. Joey agreed.

On Los Angeles Street, the person who pitches their tent next to you is your neighbor. Sometimes they choose you day after day, always getting the space beside you. Albert and Joey were always next to each other.

"He's got my back," Albert said.

People sometimes got jealous of Albert because he had such a nice tent.

Joey always defended him.

"He saved up for that tent."

Nobody got jealous of Joey, but they listened to him.

Joey had the smaller tent.

Oath

With blood on his shirt and tie, he takes the oath. The plane moves, bumping, through turbulence. Aristophanes' "The Clouds." Who still makes fun of Socrates? The Dominicans, in a Latin pun, are the Dogs of God.

The apartment is sparely furnished, in homage to William Bradford. Bradford's austerity was notable after the death of his wife, Dorothy, and the illness from which he, but few others, recovered. His retrospective account of Plymouth is still perhaps the first work of American literature, nostalgic though it may be.

I rarely turn on the lights. Planning assassinations is much easier in the dark.

One is a good number. One bed, one chair, one desk, one dresser, one toothbrush.

The file cabinets are battleship gray. They are full of information.

Power transfers at 35,000 feet.

When the plane lands, no one dies.

My desk is from the Goodwill store; everything else is new.

The President appears to fly a plane and the war seems to be over...

Sidewalks bleed; structures sweat; it's so clear now that I rule the world!

He wanted to be like the Buddhist monk in Saigon in 1963, to say something last and final about the world. He'd wandered downtown LA for ten years searching for a scarlet sunset. Perhaps ten years was enough. Jesus wandered far less time than the Israelites of Exodus. Yet, Christ not Moses is God.

Finally Donald immolated himself in Pershing Square. In broad daylight. (I've never understood that phrase, or why it's become such a standard cliché.)
It's hard to say if Donald really knew the story of Thich Quang Duc. The monk has his own memorial now in Ho Chi Minh City. And his car is on display there. At least a hundred other monks followed suit at the time.

The bus stops for him, but Lawrence does not get on the bus.

The bus driver closes the door that he had opened, cursing and muttering.

The bus is late.

Donald

The papers said that Donald served in Vietnam. But that couldn't be right. He died in the summer of 2005, the season of the Los Angeles Witch trials. He was 37 years old at the time.

Rant #2

But I get it out by this wind is pretty good at this too much fucking background noise that it may not say shit...

Wander...square...barefoot girl...round-robin...aimless statuary...water...wasted... seamless...

Blatant stop signs...rogue witness...chute yes...churches...bombed...tootsie roll blow pops...toll roads...abandoned dogs...cracked skylights...sand crepuscular...television screens...screws and nuts and bolts and nails...dead donkeys...on trains...toy store... butcher shop...beach town in shambles...cactus...dead leaves...a hole in the fabric... Louis, Charles, Henry...kings...chess games at Kang's...

Thoughts burst in bubbles separated by wire...scatterplots...dots...fits...seizures on sidewalks...taxi flat tires...red spike heel shoes...broken umbrellas...paperback books...potato chip bags...old ladies...flowers and shopping carts...Winged Victory at Samothrace...coins and threads...cardboard rain...abandoned storefronts, steel grates, shuttered windows—plywood applied, spackle and paste; parking meters bleat for more money..freeway signs speckled with graffiti, tagging crews active long after dark...Russian agents crash my apartment, the one I used to have before now...

Gravity under manhole covers... Sewers sucked to the sea... Canvas duvets...No lace, stitched well...Birdsongs warble close to the coast

Anvils fired

It can't seem to rain.

Some things are hard to know.

The Wait

She sits on the stairs and blows smoke rings that vanish misshapen into the windy night.

I see her in the crooked glow of the streetlight.

She lights another cigarette. The light of the lighter briefly illuminates her hands. Still I see mostly her forehead.

She smokes another half-dozen cigarettes. She does not know I am here. She cannot see me. It is hard for me to decide.

I do not smoke.

I have a small flask in the pocket of my jacket, and every now and then, I take a sip of rye.

At the time of the Assumption, she was mine, but what is time?

I had a hat in my bag, but I cannot find it.

Orville Wright and Gandhi died on the same day.

I always wanted to own a bird, but I never bought one.

She stops smoking. Perhaps she has no more cigarettes.

Still she does not move from her spot. Neither do I.

Parking Meters 3

A few months later, the city finishes installing the new parking meters on Los Angeles Street. The beheaded meters—once guillotined—have grown heads once again. Their new faces have flashing dials and slots for credit cards to take the car owners' payments. They have stuff inside them now.

There was no sunshine today; there is no darkness tonight. It is simply gray.

Liturgy of the Eucharist

The Holy Ones

It seems the sewage level rises always.

Beneath the ground;

Rubble atop.

A crowd.

The sound of Mass sex.

Marco wields a knife;

Flinches minimal.

Blood flow stanched.

"Better here than cardboard boxes."

"Not so."

Tits sag.

Text lifted straight from manuscript. Not illuminated.

Shipboard sermon.

Late-term pregnant girl.

Shiny silver nails on fingers and toes.

Seasick.

"Como se dice 'Porciuncula?'"

Never say "meandering river."

Cloistered nun.

Mud and concrete.

Food scraps pleasant.

Marco holds a knife to Wendy.

Instead he slits his own wrists.

No lights, no sirens.

Darkness rises, celebrated.

Twelve seats at the bar.

I want her badly.

Silent, sanctified.

Shoot, kill, torture, rape. Infect, fester, pus. War wounds. Impacted options.

Giles Corey pressed.

Recycled stone.

Shots strike rock, E. Coli.

Rockets red flare.

Dead bodies splayed.

Betty, Dahlia, Peony.

"May I buy you a drink?"

Baptized, confirmed—he has his gun.

The road to Damascus.

Torquemada.

She rejects the gun; she accepts the knife..

Smiles cut like haircuts.

She grins; you grin; they grin.

Bar lights down low.

We talk in silence while bodies mount, torn, toiled, mail unopened.

I stab; you stab; she stabs; we stab.

Bodies shredded in night light.

Cut and slash.

Bone and gristle bleed; she rends flesh.

Monica, Monica, woman of the blade.

Gate of Heaven Roman Catholic Church, South Boston, Massachusetts.

Closed for the summer.

City Blocks

Broken bottles, shattered glass.
I decry my deciduous life; I molt like a reptile.
Trash swirls and eddies in the gutters like dirty water in a drain.
She holds my hand then lets it go.
I live alone in a single room; last year I did not.
At the dark bar, spilled beer puddles on the polyurethane.
We don't know whether to stay or to leave. For a whole host of reasons.
We stay until the pungent end.
I light a cigarette; she does not smoke.
I wander the streets until dawn.
The sun is a binding document.

Detroit

I wish I could sleep in my car.

Stretch out in the back seat,

My knees just a little bent –

A blanket or two

To guard against

The cold night air,

But I do not own

What Detroit makes;

I have no car to sleep in.

Vespers

INSIDE
OUR
TENT,
PITCHED
ON
THE
SIDEWALK.

HOLDING
HANDS
IN
LINE
AT
THE
SOUP
KITCHEN.

Atoms and Strings

Atoms are points;
Strings are cellos—I don't much like violins.
Thoughts are gaps, lacunae, the spaces between:
What are the thoughts between the thoughts?
Both intellect and intolerance were begat at Cluny,
Form follows function, or perhaps function follows form;
Beauty always finishes first.
Your beauty is not mine;
Not "I think therefore I am;"
Rather, I am therefore I think.
Dark Matter exists within, not without.
Time does not go by.
Daphne could not outrun Apollo;
Not then, not now.
On idle nights, I bask in the Malibu sun —
Unknowing.
Unknown.
Wins are victories of thought;
Salamis? Plataea? Mind over matter; matter over mind—you choose.
Thinking over thinking, power over power;
The matter of hair shirts and the survival of Catherine of Aragon.
The next thing is the last thing, and the last, the next;
Knowledge fails while thought prevails.
We know not what we know.
I've not driven a car in a dozen years,
Though I'm in love with perfect circles.
Limits indeed approach zero.
Chinese food delivered to my door;
It feels like history.

I gave up meat for Lent;
I saw her on the bus,
Radiant and alone;
Dante had to be wrong,
Though perhaps right for his time,
Never, and always, immemorial:
The Second Coming begins at sunset and lasts throughout the night.

Contents of my Shopping Cart

My leg hurts today, and my feet do too. I count the contents of my shopping cart: Bottles to recycle and my blankets, two pair of worn Adidas, wet socks waiting to dry, a pocket-sized cactus plant and the dirt that spilled in my backpack; a paperback copy of "City of God," pen and paper; fountain pens, no ink; a dirty towel, an empty packet of Tide—to get the stains out, or some other such talk, damp socks and dirty underwear, a cover less copy of Plato 's Republic; Thelonious Monk Alone, three Algren books; an emptied toothpaste tube; of course— Locust and Letter.

Doubt is the Key to Faith

Doubt is the key to faith; our imperfection is our holiness; our conflicts are our sanctity. Our flaking skin becomes the universe—ashes not just ashes; dust not merely dust.

At birth and at death, all space is closed space. We move not in space, but in time, but it's the same thing, of course. One step, one mile, a light year—it makes no difference. Barefoot and shodden, naked and clothed, sick and alive, movement is movement, obstacles notwithstanding, mobility nonetheless.

Openings close as closures open, tools discarded and uses reinvented; crawling is as good as walking when the sun goes down. Night engenders night as darkness begets darkness as surely as dawn. Vibrations reign over particles and words set forth the trembling strings and thoughts trigger the words, the pictures, the images, the sentences, the scratching and the scrawling, the hunt and the chase, the snake swallowing its tail, the pursuit and the striving, the beginning and the end, and the beginning all over again.

Tarot

The Tarot cards arrived in the mail today,
Addressed to my homeless shelter.
The first one said I would live a long life;
The next one told a different story.
Bourbon kings all die young
Jokers sit by the trees.
The Magna Carta spells out all the rules,
While the rest of us wait and all freeze.
The card reader girl dresses sexy,
Her fingernails scratch at my palm;
I wait for her words to direct me,
Her skirt is layered and her feet are bare,
She wants twenty more dollars to move on.

I give her my money;
I suckle her toes.
Her feet smell like my mother's;
That much I know.

I spend the night with her.

It's all I can do.

I leave in the morning, bathed in patchouli, suspended, Brownian motion come alive, a catatonic two of clubs, staggering still, off Vine Street, before the tear-down, after the Rapture, before fulfillment had ever been known.

My shopping cart is still there, chained to the fence outside her place, locked and bound, while I and only I have the key.

With her and my cards in mind, my future determined in the faces of nobility—through the queen and the jack and the king, in red and in black, in hearts and diamonds and in clubs and spades, in my lifelines and my tea leaves, and in the grinds left in my coffee cup, and the grinds left in hers, in her feet of henna and her toes painted silver, I unlock my belongings and push the contents of my world, all in one place, along the splattered street.

The Old Days

Freshly showered at the shelter, I slipped through the crowd. Just like the old days.

No Place

No place to sit no place to sleep no place to lay down no place to settle no place to plant roots. No doorway—no diner—the noise of the night—no place to sleep. No dinner is no food, no place to sleep no place to rest. No place to be, no place to become, no place to go. No place in time, no place in place, no place to go.

No place to read, no place to sow. No place to reap, no place to die.

Jorge

Jorge takes me under his wing, but Jorge is drunk. We look for bottles and cans—in people's trash bins.

Jorge sings at the top of his lungs. He sings Al Green with an accent: "I'm So Tired of Being Alone."

He sings a narcocorrido.

The coyotes sing crazy.

Jorge's eyes bug wide: "Someone's trying to kill us!"

Coyotes howl bark whoop cry yelp chant.

Wild dogs don't bite.

Observations

A fat girl in an orange track suit, like a Creamsicle; an old Japanese man on a decrepit bicycle; janitors and cleaning ladies waiting for the bus; a white man in Armani—yes, I do know; seven people who turned me down for a quarter; one girl who gave me a dollar; buying a hot dog from a street vendor from El Salvador; ten bucks from a sweaty man driving a Porsche; phlegm spit on my face; a hot chick on a Schwinn; high heel sandals; my mother's feet; thinking of sirloin—five years back; down into the subway at Pershing Square; an old lady in a long coat; boat people on foot, bare toes splayed; Guatemalans shopping on Broadway; piñatas for sale on Olympic; cops shunting traffic on Alameda; art kids on Main Street; Bekah in jail—I think; Famous Bill holds forth on San Julian—talking to reporters about his heroic deeds; lawyers leaving the office for lunch ; neckties and nylons; giggling girls racing to Happy Hour; bottles of Night Train—and Wild Irish Rose; tourists afoot by the Biltmore; crackheads argue at the corner of 5th and Spring; a lady in an electric wheelchair runs over my foot; it hurts; on the next corner, she argues with a man on crutches; it was 50 degrees yesterday; today it is 85; I stuff my coat in my backpack; I check my pocket for my lucky quarter; now it is there; Bekah found it for me; my mother gave it to me; buses pull to the curb as cop cars screech by; a man I know talks to himself; I do not know his name; all the cars tonight are white; Detroit makes what I do not own; most places are closed; I have no friends inside these places; once I have been to Phoenix; once I have been to Oakland; twice I slept upstairs; spilled garbage smells; rabbits are rodents; just like rats; a girl in a short skirt waits to cross Main Street; she smells really nice; I have never been to Stockton; nor to Modesto; men on 6th Street ask for money; no one asks me for money; it looks like rain; also, it looks like apples and potatoes; in French, both are pommes; I can tell the guy in the wifebeater lifts weights; his girlfriend is short; a dead body in a hotel water tank; half a bottle of beer left on a curb stone; another hot girl on a bicycle; a new police station; a taco truck in Little Tokyo; a jaywalking ticket; tents and big boxes; close to home; the freeway overpass; cloverleaf and Irish luck; the lights in the hills are prettier than stars; I can't see either from where I am; ghosts hang out at gas pumps; Pentecost at the convenience store; three girls are blonde and one is brunette; Sikh men cash out Diet Coke; Pig Man; cool boy yellow castle; fast music as get; round at bed mud for winter; hot red cow; say where are funny dog?; cocoon follow sister; me hand down slow see his calendar Defoe; whale oil wolves plus tint glue-all tundra; wine glass plus paper clips; roadside chamber music; bus boys play dominoes in midnight alleys; cars double parked; one girl bigger than the other; always I thought time stopped but, no, it started; sun shines without stars; time blackens; crows alight on my clothesline—non-existent; officer of the year; pink stucco and cold beer; immemorial islands; make-up counter at the defunct department store; some parade; highest heels ; shrubs on Skid Row; coffee cups and Sharon's silver toenails; did you accuse Christmas of the crime?; thinking of the Resurrection; Bales of hay in Bakersfield ; Mick Jagger; my mother's feet; sweet pedicures—her nails pale silver; Sequoia trees older than God; loud music and long nails; lottery tickets unclaimed; television unhad and unwatched; utility bills; the notion of beauty; water and William Mulholland; obviously the fountain on Riverside; purple nail polish; helicopters overhead; no cars in the driveway; no car—no driveway; no home; coyotes clamor; bedside relief: my box—my tent; weather report; car crash; white Honda; no news at eleven; off-center; pilot light off; atoms collide; experiments accurate and awry; her platinum blonde hair; late night drinks; lost keys; places far away: the car alarm; decibels; streetlights askew: arms akimbo; nuts and cheese; the Jersey shore; flora and fauna left behind; my old apartment; hers; hair dyed red; fingerprints; broken glass; police badges and fast cars and high speed chases; my girl; jukebox at the dive bar; the Vegas strip; bad jokes; belly up to the bar; she doesn't look like me; dark night, lights out; empty bags; Kafka-esque; Patti La Belle; once, my song; my suitcase by Glad Bags; Jiffy Lube; possessions discarded; LAPD; time away; create time; Church's fried chicken; free at last; purple fingernails - polish unchipped; young and old; Dinosaur Jr.; Feel the Pain; pajama parties; desert nights; San Jacinto; late night driving; cars and trucks; love unlost;

Frederick

I want to tell you a picture in stories. The rain fell on us and we could not stop it. We had a book between us. There was the need to eat. Oh, that. And the green bottle that shattered. Jellyfish stifled beneath the cloud. Wood always points down. Long curly hair pulled up. I know what she says but I can't follow the format. Church bells. Spillage wiped dry. Billboards ask for beer. Unwanted light; darkness shines. All the best mitosis yields a daily deal at Sears. My frumpled coat. Wet with errant fire hydrant, streetlights under a microscope. Buses bark. The man in the yellow slicker hands me a hot dog. No mustard, no relish. The game ends on tonic and wings. Birdshit plunked on pavement. Girls with green fingernails. Nothing happens. The finance kids drink light beer. The loss of metaphor. Sirens silent, silent sirens. Have it your way. Headscarves warm the cockles of my heart. Audubon painted that bird, but I can't remember the name of it. I think it's bedtime but I can't know for sure. She told me the shoes had been donated. She had green eyes. Certainty still lacking. Bumped and jostled on city streets. It's still a form of contact. Better than nothing. The commercial break promotes burgers and fries. I remain hungry. Broken bottles bobble above the curbstone. The hovercraft in my mind. Superficial thrombophlebitis. The two most common forms of death in the desert are desiccation and drowning. Weighed down by heavy armor, Frederick Barbarossa drowned on the Saleph River. Some say the water was only two inches deep. With the weighty gear, the Emperor could not rise. The basement bowling alley flooded and the wood warped. Sad but true. End of story. Family fate. Once again: labor lost; no love. Love back in time. Not forward. Truly back with Bekah not fully. Daffodils out of season. Strong father figure. Gone now. Resident light. Glow not reflect. Sodden dirt, flowers grow. No swing or slide. No regrets, not nothing. Sadness waxes and wanes in dark light. Wave not particle undistinguished. Vice versa. Trucks without shocks. Clammering. The sound of the last century: clanging. The sound of this one: beeping. Gas pumps calculate. Wearing hats on hot nights. Ears covered. Faded white lines marking lanes where buses pass. Trash trucks drop their contents. Night. All ragged and invisible.

Santa Ana Winds

Something is wrong, off-kilter, askew, awry: Santa Ana winds in April, the cruelest month.

On San Julian, on Wall Street, at 6th Street, our tents and our boxes fold, collapse, blow away. Belongings dispatched, not by man, by nature, actually unusual. No trucks to confiscate, no uniforms to dictate possession.

Latch key lessons lost; I share my space with pigeons.

Soda cans, cigarette butts, cherished items: lost, lacking, longing, lace, the embroidered alphabet. No: want, wont, claimed, re-claimed.

Sidewalk stained with we know not what. Pink dress tattered.

Hot air balloons rise, but not here. Helicopters fly low. No results.

Storefront signs in Asian languages; my toy stores belong to the Japanese.

With my bedroll, I cannot comprehend commerce.

My mother let me slide down her leg, my crotch crashing on her high insteps and arches. I loved being a child.

Some parked cars wear out their welcome.

I do not know how to drive.

Truly no one to drive the car.

Full Doorway

It's morning and I have to move, but I don't want to move: not one bone; not one muscle; not one inch. I don't want to move at all.

The sun has almost risen, but there's a marine layer, and the day will be gray.

Yesterday was gray, too. And the day before.

Mr. Yamaguchi owns the toy store. I sleep in his doorway. It's small but deep and it blocks the wind. Most often he is nice to me, but he doesn't know my name. I tried to introduce myself once, but he opened his grate and he turned his back on me. Then again his English is not very good.

"You go now," he says every morning. At least five mornings, which is all I have stayed here. I was someplace else before. And somewhere else before that. Before two doorways ago, I can't remember.

It's hard to see the moon—even when it's bright. I know it's because I look at the ground.

There is a lot to see on the ground. The gum stains; the cigarette butts; the broken curbs; the potholes; the empty bags of Cheetos, of Ruffles, of Fritos; the penny, the dime, the quarter; splashes of paint; the engineer's marks for the new water main; a single shoe; tattered clothes; a solo glove; footprints; grease and oil; unnamed stains; shredded tires; a broken lamp; shards of lettuce; office memos; sticks of lipstick; wooden matchsticks; things I can use and things I cannot; civilization and detritus.

Mr. Y works his routine: opening the grate, washing his windows, pulling carts of his wares onto the sidewalk.

I work mine: I pack my things; I roll my blankets; my shopping cart is a model of efficiency.

I push the cart down the street towards Campers' Bar. They serve eggs. I have a couple of dollars. Or, almost.

I don't want to move, but I have to.

Albert's Story

Albert—

I go by Albert Green now. When I was a kid, they called me Al. When I was working, I used to go sing some karaoke. You know, like singing along. This one place I went, they'd go like, "Here comes Al Green." But, man, when I started going down, I started feeling bad. Like I was going to bring him down with me or something.

* *

I've lost my shoes. I am discalced like a Carmelite nun.

I know where to get shoes. I'll get some tomorrow.

I've misplaced my lucky quarter, the one my mother gave me. My mother would tell me to calm down—she would say "it will turn up." She was always right. Still I start to scream. Albert hugs me. I continue to scream.

A policeman walks over. He is dressed all in blue. He does not hit me. He asks what's the matter?

"My lucky quarter!" I scream. I manage to make a little sense. Usually, my screams are not words. Albert knows that.

Albert fishes in my pockets,

The policeman tells Albert to back off. The policeman raises his hand.

I call Albert by name.

"I'm not ripping him off," Albert shouts. "I'm helping him find it!"

The policeman darts his eyes back and forth between Albert and me. He backs off.

Albert has my quarter. He hands it to me. It was deep down in my pocket and I couldn't feel it. I hug Albert. I am OK now. The policeman makes sure. Then he walks away.

I don't like to lose things.

Air Time

What was time before time, before time was called time, before the word time, before the word at all, before the measurement of time, or of anything at all, before the beginning, before there was no yesterday?

John 1:1.
In the beginning was the Word, and the Word was with God, and the Word was God...

What is nothing?

Nothing is nothing. No thing is nothing.

I see birds fly, and insects, too. And planes and helicopters and other things in the air—dust mites and pollen, dirt and dust.

I see the air and I feel the air and all the things in it. Petals and leaves are in the air, too. Sometimes larger objects.

I stay on the ground.

And Joey stays on the ground and so does Albert and so does Bekah and so do I.

Joey is only staying in Albert's tent because Albert did not meet a woman tonight.

Time

Once is always and always is once. Recurrence is unique. Uniqueness recurs. Where I was once, I always am. When I'm always somewhere, I'm only there once. I'm always never been. My tent on 6th Street, then on San Julian. The windstorm blew it away, or the city officials confiscated it, removed it, took it away. It's the same to me. No more; all gone. I appear without belongings. I re-appear. Corvids are the smartest birds, breaking walnuts on the crosswalks. At the altar, the Bishop makes the sign of the Cross, the Trinity that is all things: the proton, the neutron, the electron. There's no need to count past three. Einstein understood: energy, mass, the speed of light—no more.

The police have come again. Once, twice, ten times—it doesn't matter. Just like Jesus. Don't obsess on the 2nd Coming. It doesn't matter. It's the 28th time and it's the same as the first; it's still a singularity.

I am reborn on Central Avenue.

Albert, Joey, Bekah, cops.

Trash, wind, seldom rain, infrequent. Basin and range.

If the weatherman calls it June Gloom, I think it's time to sleep, to rejuvenate, to pitch my tent on concrete or asphalt, to wake again, to rise, though the sun never really does.

Life vomits life. Ants attack gutters gracefully. Boric acid simply redirects. Replication is inexorable, orders of magnitude unimaginable, irrelevant.

I have my quarter, my blue thread, my blanket—but not my Bekah.

Regula Et Vita

I have my own rules.

I used to have other people's rules.

In jail I have their rules.

The police tell me where to move.

I do not like to move.

But I follow their orders.

Hester Prynne followed the rules.

Sometimes she did not.

I like my rules.

When I am asked to leave a Toy District doorway, I follow the rules.

But first I follow my own rules: I make sure I locate my lucky quarter; I feel my pockets for the blue thread; I call out for Bekah.

Sometimes it does not go my way.

I cannot establish the rules—at least I cannot figure where his rules end and mine begin.

I start to shout. He uses his phone. I do not have a phone. So I shout louder. He uses his phone more. I cannot leave until I work through my rules. My rules; not his. He becomes mad at me. I am not mad at him. I just want to follow my rules—my quarter, my thread, my Bekah. But my Bekah is not here. My rules fail me, break down, become absent, unworking. The toy store man does not understand me. I understand him.

I think about monasteries. This does not help me.

I ask the man about abbots and monks. This does not work either.

When the police arrive, there is a new set of rules.

I struggle to understand and I ask the officers about Cluny, about what they know.

I begin to chant "Pater Noster." My voice is pretty decent. They have not seen "From Silence to Light."

Singing so loud makes my stomach hurt. It's been some time since I have eaten.

I vomit into the gutter, splashing puke onto the sidewalk and the pavement, onto the concrete and the asphalt. This does not help me to explain my rules to them. In fact this is not one of my rules.

Their rule is to take me away. My rule is not to lose my shopping cart. My rule is that the shopping cart is me. I have me in the cart. My rule is not to lose me.

Now we have very different rules of life.

I stop singing.

I feel funny, but I know I have violated one of their rules. I just don't know which one. If it were Salem, I would know I could not dance, or go into the forest at dark, or make pies with urine.

I am at a loss here.

One policeman pushes me. I know that this is a good sign.

I thank him. He slaps me. He does not know my rules. His partner tells me to hurry up, to move along, to go away. I am happy. He knows my rules; he knows my life. I think I have seen him before. He smiles at me. I know that for a fact. I see him. His partner swats at me again but he doesn't mean to. I think he understands my rules now too.

I hurry up. I put my damp blankets in my shopping cart. I do not fold them carefully. Crumpled blankets are against my rule. But I get it. I can obey my rules later.

I push my cart, my wrinkled belongings, down the street a door or two—maybe three or four. This toy store man does not open his shop so early. I can fold my blankets there. I can count my money there, all my quarters, nine or ten, including my lucky one, or maybe excluding it; I'll have time to figure it out.

Church

I wandered out of downtown LA and out towards Griffith Park. I was looking for a church. The church had to be run by a religious order. I did not want a diocesan place. Those guys did not have the commitment I was looking for. Poverty, chastity. Franciscans, Jesuits, Augustinians. Just south of Los Feliz Blvd., Our Mother of Good Counsel had it all. I was late for mass. Nonetheless, I genuflected, and sat down in a pew. I had bummed enough money to get a six-pack of beer. By the time the priest was delivering the homily, I had to piss. I left my backpack in the pew, and went to the bathroom. By the time I got back, an explosion had occurred in the confessional. Right next to where I had sat. I had been taught not to leave before communion. But I knew I had to go. The police came quickly. I wanted to leave my backpack behind. But I knew I could not. I snuck back in to grab my bag. My lucky quarter, which my mother had given me, and my blue thread were both inside. I knew there was no way I could lose them both. Whether or not anyone had seen me. I ran south on Vermont Avenue, thinking I was victorious. I was and I was not. No one ever slips through the cracks.

Buildings

Buildings break differently from bodies;
Decomposition bubbles —
Stone crumbles;
Watching dust and sunset.
My broken arm, Sharpies sign my plaster cast;
Shadows shadow plastic bags,
Windblown near the convenience store,
Lives blasted beyond boulevards,
Wasted, in dumpsters, diving for food,
Expired by label,
Dated,
Frosted and melted.
Slides and swings,
Parks and playgrounds lost,
Last lap long gone –
Left field, left out, left-handed;
Time out, off-center,
No green grass;
Asphalt road, cheap tents, cardboard boxes, no sleep,
Dead trees;
No labor; love lost.

Cops

Shots ring out. Odd here. We're in our tents and boxes. We scatter. No surprise. We have sleeping bags and bottles of Night Train. Maybe a knife or two. I duck inside a doorway. I want to lay down on Bekah but I cannot find her. I know Mr. Yamaguchi's doorway and I go there but Bekah is not with me. Perhaps I am not her hero. Officer Patton consoles me but I know no relief. They have a man in handcuffs. I search in my pockets: my lucky quarter and my blue thread—both are still there. I can feel the quarter between my fingers and my thread at my fingertips. But I can see no one now. The policeman has left.

Graffiti pocks the grated doors. Shuttered, closed.

I want to sleep but I cannot. I'm alone. Lonely, by myself.

I can't sleep. I can't sleep without Bekah.

Now we're parted.

Questioning

It's the Iraq thing, he said. PTSD, you know. That's why I fired the shots off.

But I can't find Bekah.

Bekah?

My girlfriend!

I've never seen you with a girl.

He's lying. He knows Bekah. I don't know him. I've never seen him before.

The cops talk to me like I did it. I've never shot a gun. But I was there. They question me, interrogate me.

What were you doing?

Trying to sleep.

But you were awake?

I couldn't sleep.

So what were you doing?

Tossing and turning.

Not sleeping?

No.

Do you own a gun?

Own?

Possess.

(Do they want to take my shopping cart?)

I do not understand, I say.

I mean it.

Did you go to mass last week?

What?

Church?

Yes…I like to go to church.

What church do you go to?

What?

Which church?

Which church?

Yes.

I don't know.

What do you mean you don't know.

Roman Catholic.

That's not what I mean.

You're a police officer?

Yes.

I'm lost here.

Let me bring you back.

Ok.

Do you remember the bombing?

No.

Let me refresh your memory: a man with a backpack blew up the confessional booth at Our Mother of Good Council last week.

Oh.

That's all you have to say?

In nomine patri et filiis et spiritu sancti.

What?

I blessed myself.

Were you there?

There?

At the church?

Do you know where Bekah is?

Excuse me?

My girl.

As far as we know you don't know any girls.

Excuse ME!

We're talking about bombs and bullets here !!!

I'm not following you.

We have cameras.

I used to have a camera. It got stolen. Can you find it? I have pictures of Bekah on my camera.

What are you talking about?

Bekah!

I think we should let this guy go, one officer says.

I'm interrogating him!!!!

We're wasting our time!!!

Do you want to see my lucky quarter?

The tough officer slaps me.

I am free to go.

Filament

They say vibrating strings are the building blocks of nature. I studied filaments: hair, a piece of stamen, protein, bacteria, the wire in an incandescent bulb. I keep my blue thread in my pocket.

The buildings here seem taller than they used to be. Their shadows make it dark, darker.

Bekah's shadow is beside me. We walk hand in hand. I know it is not her ghost because she is not dead. Aside from life and death, shadows and ghosts are just the same.

Cotton Mather may have become more irrelevant and increasingly vilified, but spectral evidence has grown and multiplied.

Witches hang.

The Court of Oyer and Terminer has separated me from my Bekah. Not never more.

I burned my shadow last night. We lit a fire in a trash can. Right at the corner of San Julian. Albert, and Joey and me. The fire began slowly, then grew bright.

The building block of nature is fate. Yet it's not as it seems because fate is just another story and—though there is no such thing as time—story creates time, creates forwards and backwards, events and occurrences, the telling and the re-telling, even the condemnation of silence.

The fire died out. Joey and Albert fell asleep. I remained standing, rubbing my hands together above the embers, the extinguished flames, and I watched the sun rise, my head tilting upward as my eyes followed the trajectory of the expanding brightness.

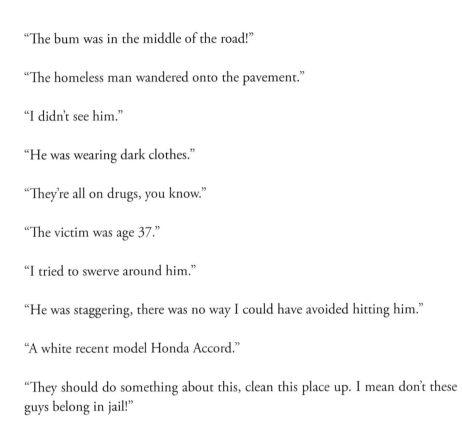

Operation Clean Sweep

"The bum was in the middle of the road!"

"The homeless man wandered onto the pavement."

"I didn't see him."

"He was wearing dark clothes."

"They're all on drugs, you know."

"The victim was age 37."

"I tried to swerve around him."

"He was staggering, there was no way I could have avoided hitting him."

"A white recent model Honda Accord."

"They should do something about this, clean this place up. I mean don't these guys belong in jail!"

"The unidentified indigent is in critical, but stable, condition at County USC Medical Center."

Redacted

I xxxxxx the money xxxxx on the counter xxxxx the 7-11....I left my hat on the xxxxxxx, replete with xxxxx.... Radios blasting xxxxxx dumpsters full of xxxxx expired xxxxx barely two xxxx old. Middle xxxxx bombs xxxxx a xxxxxx of children .... Grime under my xxxxxx .... Rumpled clothes xxxxx suspended in the rain....openly associates with Syrian nationals on the xxxx of Los Angeles .... Trying the doors of xxxxx cars left overnight near xxxxxx, tents and boxes full of sleeping xxxxx, police patrols suspicious of xxxxxx, three homeless men xxxxx, studying bus routes, xxxxx traveling xxxxx, inside rank xxxx apartment buildings xxxxx, uncut hair xxxxx of blood, rants about xxxx and preachers; suspected xxxxxx conspiracy .... Hallucinatory visions of the Holy Roman Empire in the xxxx Ages, conflicts arisen over xxxxxx succession, interrogators dispatched to xxxxx in order to question xxxxx .... Use of force xxxxx. Up against a graffitied wall xxxxx yields little xxxxx except a run-down of the Investiture xxxx, citing xxxxx named Gregory and xxxxx, and xxxxx about xxxxx and xxxxx, and asking forgiveness in the middle of a snow xxxx. Released on xxxxx xxx recognizascence with xxx warning... All attempts exhausted to find a xxxxx gun...Public Works sweeps the xxxxx streets outside the barbed wire xxxxx, crows xxxxxx on the wire.... City workers ignore the xxxxx birds.

Charges dropped against the xxxxx. Operation Clean Sweep authorized to .... syringes swept under local xxxx, confiscated xxxxx bedrolls stored under Court Order in locked xxxx bins, accessible only with xxxx.

This xxxxxxx population xxxxx the value of downtown xxxxxx according to numerous reports provided by the xxxxx of xxxxx.

Historical research into the Investiture xxxxx shows xxxx links with the current xxxx acts of vandalism and xxxxx.

The contents of the belongings, stored in xxxxx, revealed no further or additional xxxx.

Things

Things are my life but not those things. I cannot buy things. I am with things. Things are not alive, things that are not alive.

I have my thread and my quarter today but not just my things. My things are few: they drape my body; they fit in my backpack or my cart when I have one. On a good day, my best things are in my pocket. They live though they are not alive. I take care of them and watch over them and check on them all the time. Some days I count to ten and reach into my pocket to see if they are still there, then I count to ten again and do the same thing, and over and over. I feel better and time passes. Yes, I know: there is no such thing as time. Time is not a thing. I shouldn't have said it that way. But I did and it is done, though nothing is ever done, ever finished, but everlasting.

But the sidewalk is a thing, and the pavement and the asphalt, and the storefront steel grates, and the iron bars, and parking meters and the coins inside them, stored inside their metal bellies like marsupials in their pouches, though kangaroos and platypuses are not things but something else like me.

But my shoes are things and my socks are things, and my broken pen and my tattered copy of the Iliad and the shattered glass and the cars and the buses and the crushed curbstone and the styrofoam cups and the shreds of failed tires and the plastic bags and the items on sale at the store.

And the Los Angeles Times and the police revolver and cell phone carcass and the empty cup of Coca Cola and the van and the baton and the things that hit me and the things they carry away.

Nothing but things, all things, everything. Objects of both scorn and desire. My constituent life.

I am outside of most things: I am outside of buildings and of cars and of light bulbs and of taxis and of refrigerators and of this and of that and of these things and those things and of wires and streetlights. No phone calls, no visits no letters, no emails—though these are not things but merely made by things, of things, with things, for things, through things.

I do not think of myself as a thing; I do not think I am a thing—though I know I have things inside me. I know some of those things but not others: I know magnesium and iron and copper and manganese. I know the small rock I hold in my palm and then swallow because I want to. I know the stone is old and I know that I have an old thing inside me now. I know it does not live but that it lived inside me. And I know that it will leave me, do me part. I can always eat another rock tomorrow. Of course, according to my method, it will never end. Ingest without digestion; excrete unchanged. Perhaps minuscule erosion— immortality nonetheless.

Nothing Follows Nothing

Nothing follows nothing—like lemmings off a cliff.

Zero by zero: I miss Bekah.

Blue bicycles dodge DASH buses.

Despite the rejection of my thesis, I remain committed to my theory of modernity.

Bekah lost her shoes last week. Her feet look really quite good when they're bare. Then she cut her toe on broken glass. Mishaps never help.

The Hundred Years' War still stands out in my mind.

Someone bought our hotel at 7th and Main, the Lucretia Hotel, twenty a night. They papered our doors, shoving their notice under the crack that lets in the light. It doesn't matter much; we only get to stay here once or twice a month. And now it's just me. I don't know where Bekah is.

Time beats back nothing; time's nowhere in sight. I see time on the street—trash and broken glass; cigarette butts—I see time all the time. I contain multitudes. Bekah's not here. But I sense that she will be. Nothing has past. Nothing has passed.

I see the edge of time's rot: the barefoot girl seated beside me—checks deposited, EBT, electric money—no end to the end.

Mothers and Crows

Crows crow and peck in fights in front of me. The smartest birds quarrel most. Black silhouettes grace me in forgotten shadows as I recall my shadow's immolation. Buddhist protesters enthralling generations…Fire breeding fire breeding desolation breeding life. The high arch of my white mother's tan brown feet. My birth cesarean without the passage, without the hard-fought entry into the nubile world. Salamis first; forget Thermopylae—always Plataea. But remember to celebrate the other side. A hundred crows gather on the wires across from the sidewalk that pins me to its hardness, its durability, its origin in rock and stone. The ravens flip and flap, caw and croak, their mobility posed against my stillness—motion, movement; they aggrieve their life in ways that I do not. Yet if I throw a pebble into their midst they will scatter in a fear I will never know. Or perhaps I will. I do not wish to disturb them and I do not. I bring breakfast to my mother in bed. Her voice is both soothing and disapproving. Her coffee is cold. I make her another cup. I want to make her happy; I need to make her happy; I make her happy. I do everything she asks of me.

The Roslyn Hotel has a television in the lobby. I am not a guest but they let me stay in the lobby until 8 PM. I have a thermos and I drink water from it. A sports team is winning a game. Perhaps the team is named the Ravens, called the Ravens; I am not sure; I cannot tell.

* *

I do not see any birds on the screen and I tell the bartender so. He smiles and he walks away. We do not mean the same thing. I want to say so, but I do not have any words. Words are like reaching for coins or dollars; sometimes they're just not there.

I have three dollars and the barkeep gives me one more beer. My memory's not

166

so good anymore but I think the Bud Light is only two twenty five, so I am still able to tip. Perhaps he will remember that; maybe I will, too.

* *

In the summers, I would massage my mother's feet every day. She worked at a donut shop and she said she was on her feet eight hours a day and that her feet were sore. She was happy then and I was happy. I don't think I've ever been happier. I still have the lucky quarter she gave me. It's in my pocket. I better check to see. Yes, yes, it's still there.

I decide to throw a rock into the midst of the crows. A flock is the right word, yes? I think it is. A pride of lions, a litter of pups, a flock of crows... A bevy of something, a bushel of another, a gaggle of geese, a pack of wolves, a den, a school, a pod, a herd.....and so on and so on.

I throw the stone, a pebble really, not to hurt, not to harm, but, yes, to scatter, to disturb, to disrupt... To make something, anything, just go away..."I'm in charge," I shout. The birds dutifully fly away, but now I am alone.

Heat

It's hot as shit and even if I had a tent I wouldn't sleep in it. Something's over; I'm just not sure what it is. I always feel beginnings and endings but not middles— or maybe the other way around. I'm not so sure.

So that I can stay the night they want to test my blood. It might be cherry red. I don't really care.

Everybody wants a piece of something.

Tree roots crack sidewalk concrete fissures erupt in stone, codes of law entrenched, uneven surfaces... Buckled vertically...Hard to settle down... Difficult to sleep...Pack up strip down...hide...Become lost from view... I sweat strip search swim stretch seek strive beyond the place I sleep...The things I have, the things I don't...

Point Blank

Point blank

From Sunday

Scattered—

The essential quality

Of the universe

Has no geometry –

Point taken

Not lost:

Puff of air

Formless pulse

The sounds we make

Both ephemeral

And permanent—

Burned blades of grass

Insufferable twilight—

I've waited with patience

For the cock to crow.

Rest

I tuck myself in to sleep.

I lay down to sleep or I lie down to sleep.

I try to sleep.

I nestle down in the doorway to sleep.

Paper, scissors, rock.

The doorway where I sleep is shuttered and locked tonight.

Pebbles and stones, sand and grit: I pray my rosary without fail.

Nuestra Señora, my lady, my virgin, my Queen of Angels, ruler of the River, mortgage of my soul; street names pass me by; the swamp, the fleas, the tar pit, Governor Pico, adobe and steel, General Motors, and strip clubs; the Virgin wears no clothes. Innocent evil. The worst kind.

Leftover hot links stir my soul.

I try hard to dream at night, tonight, every night.

I can't find Bekah. I never can. I always will.

My dreams fail me. Always do.

It's July and it's nine at night and it is still light and I cannot sleep and I cannot find a place to lay down, to lie down, and I move on, and I walk and I push my cart and I leave it behind and I find it again but something's missing and I try to find what's gone and I cannot remember and I check my pockets and my blue thread is there and my lucky quarter is there and I cannot remember what is not there but I know it is gone, and I miss it, and I know that I do, though I don't know what it is and then I find a place to lie down, to lay down, and then it is dark and then there is no one around and then I am tired and then I check my pockets again and then I push my cart near to my feet so I can feel it, feel the metal—I unscrew the wheels with a wrench that I happen to have—and then I settle down and then I try to dream and then I fail and then it's better and then it's worse and then perhaps I sleep.

There is no such thing as rest.

Larry Fondation

Stations

I take no vows. Once I was in; now I am out. Asteroids strike, implode, explode, expel. Exclusion, expulsion. Once I am expelled, how do I include?

Re-inclusion? Is re-absorption a real possibility?

Motion and location cannot both be determined. I do not stay in one place—not for long. But nor can it be said that I really move.

I stay on 6th Street, on Town, on San Julian, on San Pedro; I drink at Campers' Corner, at the park on the corner, in front of the police station; I move to the Mission; I stay on Wall Street, at the bus stop, at the train station, at wherever they will let me.

Sixtus

Seamless robe, turbulent heretic—

I scatter my own ashes.

Seasons hardly rage yet the temperate gives way to palaces of plenty,

Awash in the hydrants of the lone apostate,

Scrambling for cover along streets of cacti and asphalt,

Concrete and cement,

Crows and barbed wire.

In the name of the aforementioned we pray.

Without light, light;

Without darkness, darkness.

I drink from plastic cups, newspapers undistributed—

Among stone pillars and undulating poplars,

Vestments disheveled, secluded areas scheduled for deforestation;

Walking briskly through battered buildings

To find the manger reinvented.

Alexander

It ended at exactly midnight,

All the pomp and circumstance,

Everything we stood for;

The ramparts shredded,

The banners torn;

No one likes withstanding loss,

Even though we often do;

Purple sunsets fail my eyes —

Always open,

Closure not an option.

Sing - song freeway no relief;

Absence of winter no comfort,

Duty-bound,

Cold soup in closet queues

While unwelcome guests abound;

Trial by fire, trial by stone,

Civil power withdrawn,

The inquisitor once more reborn;

The Borgia pope a distant lust,

Memories redrawn,

Standing vanquished, pride unknown.

Centuries turn, time unfounded;

Most of us, most of all,

Dumbfounded in the awkward night;

Across the board, expelled in shadow,

Lost in tattered quest, heeding unknowledge and bad advice;

Every Cassandra a street corner madam of thwarted ambivalence;

My Girl; My Girl—the melody unsustained,

Groping for next to nothing,

Lilacs dead, unbloomed,

Sorrow nothing but an empty cup;

Sun, then rain.

Tents protect; cardboard boxes soak.

Bedrolls wet:

Homeless either way;

She tries to hold me—standing, seated, supine;

I step out of our wood pulp home to feel the night.

Conjugal

I lie for truth.

Exile is home.

My place is no place; no place is my place.

To banish me is to include me.

To ban me is to embrace me.

To embrace me is to exclude me.

I top from the bottom.

Nixon was a peacemaker.

Gandhi was a warrior.

My skin is a boundary.

My skin is porous.

Semi-permeable is a virtue; osmosis a victory.

Rights are wrong.

Responsibilities are virtuous.

Virtue is tedious.

When you simply cannot.

Cannot do.

Anything.

Necessity is unnecessary.

Addictions are required.

Elegies are pageantry.

Atoms absorb.

Molecules exclude.

Particles fail to participate.

Pauli excludes; Heisenberg is uncertain.

Strings vibrate.

My home moves.

From one place to another.

Plato punked Homer.

The blind guy won.

A cave would be fine right now.

Bend don't break.

My mother told me.

Time Is the Longest Distance

Theorem after theorem.

World unproven.

My backpack expands like the universe.

It begins as a tiny, dense dot.

My books, my socks, my only towel:

Now more than ever.

Maoists love me.

Daisies bloom.

Potholed asphalt undoes my bus.

Waiting for the next one.

Time never passes.

Sunset skyline.

Zero lot line.

Nothing comes.

Fires rage.

I walk upright.

She cut her hair off.

I cannot swim.

Nobody married.

The Maypole unshorn.

Foreign territory.

Absent asylum.

Borders ablaze.

Jailed deported.

Vacant buildings.

Neighbors gone.

Vibrant curbstone.

Muted palette.

Abetting darkness.

Monastic routine.

Pater Noster.

Run amok.

Shattered streetlights:

In Imago Dei.

Soup kitchens.

Two police cars.

Blank screen; blank slate; tabula rasa:

Hungry.

Stolen merchandise.

Hungry.

Objects alive.

Blankets have minds of their own.

My blanket has a mind of its own.

Lovely.

Reconstituted ash.

Un-enlivened.

Hungry.

Hollowed out.

A hole in the ground.

Atoms collide.

Autocrats' autumn.

Always.

Ever.

Hungry still.

Unabated.

Unabashed.

Bekah's Feet

Her feet are dirty, but shapely;

I no longer worry about dirt.

She still wears a toe ring;

I can see its faded shine—

I stare at the ground a lot,

I see things there:

Gum stains, broken shadows, chipped cement, the detritus of time,

Thousands of footprints that make no mark.

Bekah's feet strike poses in the shattered light,

Slim ankles, high arches, cracked heels;

The other men on San Julian pay no mind—

Most of us still stare at the sky.

Fires burn, but east of here,

While bombs drop in other places,

As music plays a distant tune,

Begun perhaps in Thermopylae—

Distinctive sounds imperceptible,

Whether in victory or defeat.

Months later it's time to caress Bekah's feet,

In doorways first;

In boxes second;

Next in tents—

Once at the Roslyn Hotel,

A room uncleaned, a room neglected,

A room of ours,

Nonetheless—

Space misunderstood,

Confused with time,

Cut short truly,

But impressed on memory,

On memory as a story,

On story supreme, cheaper than Walmart,

More precious than gold;

Whatever I've lost, I remember;

I remember immortal—

Achilles and Ajax, Beowulf and Chaucer, the Borgias and Dante,

And Bekah's feet;

I still have Bekah's feet,

Except when she is away from me.

Operation Clean Sweep—

Separation anxiety,

When she leaves the room;

My mother does,

But not for long.

Now it's long —

I can't tell how long.

I can't tell time.

But long is long;

Footprints are permanent,

History truncated,

Memory invincible,

Unvanquished,

Unlost.

It's not like my keys;

I still have my keys,

Which unlock nothing,

Time Is the Longest Distance

My last apartment,

My past apartment —

I cannot remember it,

Not its bathroom, nor its stove;

Not its closet, or its doorway;

I have forgotten the meaning of "when."

Some time ago,

Some space ago,

A while ago,

Then, not now—

A time ago,

Back in the day:

Ha! I have a sense of humor!

Don't you agree?

Time is a tunnel that doesn't exist;

I'm simply below the surface,

Or perhaps beneath.

The room at the Roslyn did not have a bathroom,

But it had its own sink.

I told Bekah I adored her;

I thought of washing her feet first,

But I decided to kiss them first,

Before the water, before the cleaning;

I kiss her insteps;

I kiss her toes, her soles, her heels,

The tops of her feet again;

White patches part the dirt where my lips make contact with the flesh of her feet,

I can taste her dirt in my mouth,

Her dirt;

It belongs to her now,

And now to her and to me,

The dirt of the one I love.

The room is full of the dirt of others;

I block the others from my mind.

Up on the shabby mattress, I kiss her lips;

I lick her neck, remove her shirt—

She reaches for me;

We make love.

When we've finished, I take off my T-shirt, run it under the water of a tiny, corroded sink down the hall,

Time Is the Longest Distance

And I wash Bekah's feet —

I take my time,

I use the T-shirt, the water, my tongue;

I am thorough,

I am meticulous;

I work like a monk hand-copying the Bible.

Bekah smiles, she touches herself, she falls asleep;

I crawl into the single bed beside her.

In the morning, the manager raps on the door;

He tells us it is time to leave.

He threatens to call the police.

We leave.

Outside Bekah is barefoot:

The dirt comes back.

It clings to her feet again.

I watch it accumulate as we walk,

Holding hands.

I remember being happy.

Relationships

Relationships exist before matter. They are the first thing. The Big Bang was the pre-ultimate intimate relationship. Cuddled tight. Really tight. I have few relationships. That's why I am so afraid.

Relationships occur a priori; things are borne from relationships. Ice is in a relationship with water, which in turn is in a relationship with steam. Then comes H2O. Then comes what we know. Properties and characteristics, such as cold and hot.

In the Beginning was the Word, and the Word was relationship—the signifiers and the signified. How else would we know?

Then proceeds story and it is story I try to tell. But my mind is off—the neurons out of relationship—and story I cannot tell.

I say this to the counselor at my shelter but he tells me to take my pills. I have no relationship with my pills, so I do not listen to him.

I have one old story and two new stories: my old story is my lucky quarter; my new stories are my blue thread and Bekah.

I am afraid of losing them all.

When I tell the therapist about my quarter, he says it is just an object; he says I should sever my ties. He says it is just a thing. I tell him that's not true. It is not a separation object, I say. It is my relationship with my mother. Of course it resides in an object, I say. But the quarter is no longer an object; it is a relationship that is contained, captured, confined within an object. It's like transubstantiation. He will have none of it.

He asks about breast feeding. I was never attracted to her breasts, I say. I always loved her feet.

Even at that, I say, that is not why I am here.

I want to talk about my blue thread. He doesn't seem interested. Nor in my theories about the universe.

It's the same thing, he says.

He is wrong.

He gives no thought to rescue, or saving things from destruction.

Odd for his field, I think.

I am glad when our time is over.

I want to talk about time, but I know he does not.

I will talk about time with my friends at Camper's Corner.

I would talk to Bekah if I could find her.

McDonald's: Mickey D's

McDonald's at Central Avenue and Olympic: I walk on foot to the drive-in window. Change only: ten quarters, twenty dimes, the rest pennies. Oh, and one nickel. Meal Deal #1: Big Mac, fries and Coke. Eat quickly outside. Never go inside. No refills. Discard trash in proper place: barrel provided by management, Golden Arch logo embossed in plastic.

French fries mushy: potatoes like paste. Ice melts in cold weather.

I chew the plastic straw.

It's just spit,

Spooned like sugar,

Clumps on the sidewalk,

Gathered like herds of cows,

Diet Coke,

Flocks of geese,

Formation overhead;

No ice,

Water ungathered,

Molecules dispersed,

Time Is the Longest Distance

I make noise when I swallow.

Reverse peristalsis when I vomit,

Coagulate at the curbstone,

While I wait for the bus,

Un-coming;

Delusional on mass transit,

It all rushes by:

Asphalt, pavement, storefront signs,

Over and above,

Up and over,

Left and right.

Smashed atoms yield scattered light;

City demurred,

Backwards in time,

All unwashed,

Darkness undiminished,

Two bites left

Of the burger I paid for,

Three soggy French Fries,

One ice cube,

Left in my cup,

Suck and chew,

All that's left;

Everything remains,

Brownian motion,

Excited atoms,

Widows and perverts,

Commingled at Agincourt,

Exhalation of Kings;

Coronation at dusk,

When the sun is nowhere

To be found.

I steal the schoolboy's baseball bat,

No games unplayed,

For lack of a quorum,

Or proper equipment;

Sweat unmeasured,

Sputum dripping from my chin;

I am hungry still —

Still is measured time,

Not lack of movement;

Both sides lack truth,

Or hold truth dear,

So hard to tell.

Cacti

Son of the Virgin Queen,

I crave Spanish gold;

Police arrive,

Mise en scene,

Captured, caught,

Plantagenet profile,

Hutu border,

Crossing the River Styx

Closer to midnight,

Crossing guards in highlight yellow,

Stopping traffic,

Wearing vests in Day-Glo orange,

Vineyards shorn of ripened grapes,

Peloponnesian battles

Of love lost in strict engagement,

Fought forever,

In fields of succulents,

Spiny cactus hindering progress;

Minus the night—

Beauty-bound, lacking glory,

Saguaro sentinels in the morning light:

Desert rats die for my sins.

Skid Row bar:

Nanette has dirty hands,

Cleansed by the Church of England,

Washed by Thomas More,

License expired,

Time to renew;

Fourth in line at the shelter,

Soup kitchens expanding exponentially —

My hands touching hers;

Spiders casting webs

Across the Hundred Years' War

Aiming at atoms

And subatomic particles,

Waves crashing on British beaches,

Littoral shores,

Clambakes in Boston,

Decreed by the Governor,

Pasty skin,

Never-ending night;

Rigged up like desert soldiers,

Infrared targets in evening rust,

Dust,

Like rosé wine,

Somewhere in between;

Lacking substance,

Soldier on.

I want no more,

Nothing else;

In my fecund imagination

This indoor cemetery contains no one but the dead.

Concrete and Asphalt

Concrete you,

Asphalt me;

Wilted flowers,

Central Avenue,

Sirens, horns;

Rock formations —

We stand the test of time.

Cigarette butts in Albert's tent,

Backlog in processing claims,

Application denied;

Somnambulant on street corners,

Sun neither setting nor rising

Like a gray flannel suit;

I would watch the Fall Season

If I had the means.

I know my body is a colony;

My bacteria outweigh me,

Still I have no power:

After all,

Athens lost to Sparta,

Despite their advantages,

Despite their rhetoric,

Despite philosophical prowess;

Silenced in a courtroom of my peers,

I gape at sea level swarms of plankton,

Longing for their company—

Mouth wide open.

Rejection in the form of injection,

Only when I get loud;

In the open field of alleged freedom

All the stores are closed.

Metal grates

Steel bars

Iron padlocks

Shuttered shut

Undercover of night

Plain clothes policemen,

Hiding their badges

Beneath the shattered streetlight,

Shedding darkness on nothing,

Poker chips neither gained nor lost.

Winged Victory

Nighttime noise; notes played; splayed bodies asleep on concrete; asphalt poured by monster trucks; sounds resonate quickly in vacant nights; the girl upstairs; angry afternoons; lottery season; shelters full; Powerball drawing; Seven-Eleven; not nearby; Gallo Port; barefoot girls ; shaken, not stirred; or vice versa; eviction notice; tucked under the fragrant door; wind inside; spider's web; hornet's nest; Bishop to Rook 3, or Room 3; no one knows for sure; City jail; County lock-up; same thing; Holy Ghost; time changes nothing; Cain is Abel, and Abel is Cain; time runs out, but time means nothing; out means less; luggage packed tight; the trip's around the corner: sitting on stoops, Irish Setter; large dog, silent at dawn, talked out; sworn officers swearing like sailors, clichés acknowledged—police again: sweep the streets; friends unknown; lichens and moss— cancel thoughts; cancelation is the origin of the universe; displacement unwelcome , inevitable , inexorable , ineluctable—thoughts of sleep and breakfast; recycling steel and plastic—cans and bottles quenching thirst; dark streams of piss, human and animal, all the same; the same thing over and over; the shroud and the crypt; the victory at Samothrace; battle over: hard fought.

Hard to sleep; not till morning; not then; not now. Buoys bobbing oceanside; smart gulls scarfing nutrition; calories lost to changes in moon tides; waist-high—flood oncoming; drought distended; bellies bloated; Corvids crack walnuts on crosswalks; watching the changes of lights, red to green and back again, yellow notwithstanding; orange trees vacated: we make way—we're good at making way; moving out of the way; getting out of way; told to " get the fuck out of the way;" in any case, I move— unpacked shopping cart re-packed; the clock stops before dawn; I know it well; it's over now; I struggle with vocabulary; I understand the end. It is not the end.

The end never begins, and the beginning never ends; all time is no time; neither start, nor finish; end run; opposite field; safe at home; no home; cardboard box; canvas tent; Gallo Port; bottle full; bottle gone; two cents for glass; one for metal; paper, scissors, rock. Night-blind amidst sparrows; pigeons peck the popcorn; never is the night.

Microbes 2

I ate this morning; yesterday I didn't. My microbes have always outweighed me, even at birth, so I don't worry about germs. The food they discard at Ralphs on 9th Street is good, high quality, the lettuce a bit brown, the meat a little gray. I do not take raw meat; I have no place to cook. Joey told me about camps by the river, but I am scared to go there. They say you can walk down the concrete banks, built by the Army Corps of Engineers, down by Frogtown; I read about it on the computers at the downtown library, the Richard J. Riordan Central Library, the place I am at now, but I have never been to Frogtown. I've always wanted to travel. My mother wanted to take me places, but we could not afford to go. At home, just the two of us, I took care of her as best I could. She always took care of me. From my spot at 6th and San Pedro, Frogtown seems far away, though I know it is not. The cold cuts at Ralphs are the best—sliced turkey expired, but fine. Date stamped six days ago carted out to the loading dock, discarded, separated into two stacks: one set for the shelters—good publicity, donations appreciated; the other aimed at the dumpster, too discolored to give away, but still good enough to eat. Unable to get away, my mother and I stayed close, cuddling on the couch, and watching movies on TV. I would make her snacks—pizza on English muffins, cheese plates; I'd pour her beer in tall glasses or cups of red wine. Sometimes she would let me have some; other times, quite a bit. We laughed when we got drunk. We fell behind on the rent. The donut shop never paid her much. One time I wrote a computer program to pay the bills. Money never happened often. The second time that it did, I took her shopping: we bought her two dresses—one short, one long; a pair of strappy sandals, and a sterling silver toe ring. Indeed, we never made money again. The discarded turkey has that strong poultry smell, but it tastes fine. I'd stolen some small packets of mayonnaise and mustard from Clifton's Cafeteria, which I keep in a baggie, so they don't leak onto my copy of the *Iliad* or on my few clean clothes. I tear open two packs and make a Dijon mayo from the single servings, condiments to go, useful now. I tear the brown leaves from the head of lettuce and I wrap the turkey and the mustard and the mayonnaise inside. On the benches outside the Fashion Institute, my meal is muy bueno, as Alfonso taught me to say. My mother was afraid of germs, though I learned not to be. If I dropped some popcorn while I was bringing her midnight snacks, I was glad to eat it off the floor. I wanted her to eat pristine. She chastised me at first, wanted me to throw it away, but I persuaded her that waste was bad. She taught me not to throw food away. Eventually she was pleased that I had listened to her. I learned to love her leftovers. I eat all the turkey and the whole head of lettuce, minus the core, which I cannot chew. Bacteria do not bother me. I believe they merely add to the billions inside me. Physically, I rarely get sick. The security guy patrols the loading docks where the discards and the dumpster reside. I want to light a cigarette—I have two left—but the guard asks me, orders me, tells me, to leave. I comply. My mother was a big woman—I don't think she's died but she is old now, at least—maybe she needs me—but I am not there, and she is not here. I wish I knew. The past tense is never correct, knowledge always lacking. Both dresses fit her nicely. The short one showed off her thighs, thick and strong, standing all day on the job, pouring coffee, serving sweets. The shoes fit perfectly—something to wear when we went out to dinner, to get her away from the house, time out and time off. I can't get to the discards at Ralphs the next day; the guard seems to be hanging out there. I have to come up with another plan. Of all that we bought for my mother on our shopping spree, the toe ring was the best of all.

We thought a lot about the toe ring. Sterling silver, it fit perfectly on the second toe of her right foot. She asked me if I worried if her feet were dirty. I eased her mind about germs. Very dirty, her feet were perfect. I've always had good instincts about making things clean. I eat blemished peaches from the grocery store discards. I don't mind that sweetness has gone bitter. When I massaged her feet at night, I would remove the toe ring so as not to lose it. It fit snugly, but not tightly. The plums are fully rotten. I do not take them, and I do not eat them. When I removed my mother's shoes every night, I could see the bulge of the toe ring through her socks or her hose. I was careful removing her footwear. I comb through a great deal of zucchini tonight...both wrapped in plastic and loose. It is thoroughly spoiled and rotted. I would sit on the floor and massage my mother's tired feet after work. Most nights of the week. According to her work schedule—sometimes at six o'clock, more often at seven or eight, sometimes as late as ten. The peaches fill me up, but the high from the sugar will not last. I move on and stand outside a sushi place, secretly craving protein. I sat on the floor; my mother sat on the couch. We watched a movie then another, old and new. A man outside the sushi joint hands me a bag of leftovers; the bowl inside the bag is full of white rice, nothing else. I thank the guy but throw the rice away while he is not looking. I know I don't need more starch. My mother never married. She'd never had a wedding, nor a ring. A woman tells me she has spicy tuna. She asks if I like hot food. I take the bag of food, and thank her. I slip around the corner and eat in the shadows of the nearby parking lot. I like my privacy. I sit in parking space number 109. The sushi is perfect, spicy tuna on crispy rice, and the rice crisps are still lukewarm.

Pizza Box

An empty pizza box sits atop the trashcan: I know because I opened it.

Beneath the box, the rancid garbage reeks: …stale tobacco, spoiled fish, wilted lettuce, rotted plants, animal flesh decomposing in sodden moonrise, escaping in solids and liquids and gases, all escaping at dawn like prisoners without guards, fleets of warships in forgotten harbors, obsolete before birth, stretchmarks visible in open fields: unguarded, unprotected, saturated as rice paddies, rain as good as sheltering sun, withering to unclothed skin, equally and notwithstanding, unprotected under streetlights, SPF unneeded: what wilts rises, heliotropic beneath drunken skies.

When night ends I am still hungry.

Destination Nowhere

Destination nowhere, annunciation unappreciated; walking unassisted, time explodes from fallen apples, crawling from shuttered grate to shattered glass, doors closed, windows unopened; discarded sandwich known to sidewalk preachers. I long to assemble broken furniture, laid out on the curb like candles on an altar.

I take Bekah's hand. It is just before dawn. Her eyelids droop like fishing weights. I've only gone fishing once. I think I was seven. Or maybe ten. Danger rings like church bells. Scourge strikes cluttered sidewalks, gyre unbound. I have money. I guide Bekah to breakfast. We can afford poached eggs. Walking west, we line up at the Pantry. After a short wait, we sit at the counter. I have not showered for days. Our waitress asks no questions. We change our minds and order American cheese omelets. We eat slowly on purpose. So as not to appear hungry. We ask for ketchup. It does not come in little packets. It comes in red plastic bottles, bottles we can squeeze, and we use it liberally. The potatoes come along with the eggs and we cover the hash browns with ketchup too.

I kiss Bekah and no one stares. We laugh when she spills coffee on the empty plates. Coffee is cheap here. The waitress takes our plates and refills our coffee cups. We use lots of cream, small packets of half and half. I have enough cash for a ten percent tip. Not much, but a tip nonetheless.

We leave, walk out, onto 9th Street. I have Bekah by the hand. I turn west, but I don't know what's there, what's in that direction, where the fuck to go. Instead I spin Bekah back around—head east, not west.

Time shrinks like sautéed onions, cooking down, cooking off, shrinking, substance burning off—wait long enough until there's only minor matter in the pan, charred and burned, not much left.

I know where to sleep near the corner of 6th and San Julian.

When Midnight Rings

Rocks seldom move; semi-mobile in mobile earth; tectonic shifts, oceanic plates; littoral ecology in rising tides: my fate belongs to the time when the oceans recede, to the moment when mollusks raise their molten shells, movement slight, gains large, as plankton float, not swim, buffeted about to their eventual fate, bejeweled as a queen at the court of Macbeth, or Buckingham palace—all moments depending on the changing of the guard; the head of Thomas More, the baby's rattle; we all cry when midnight rings.

Bekah and I are third in line. When we become the first, the assistant pastor tells us they are out of food—no soup, no sandwiches, no chocolate chip cookies, no beds, no breakfasts, no lights, no darkness, no meat, no potatoes, no rest, no red, no blue, no hair, no books, no gray, no sound, no bus, no stop, no clock, no thoughts, no wisdom, no ants invading, no armies, no night, no nada, no radio, no signal, no car, no train, no bus, no night.

We don't eat; we don't fight; we go back; back to where: back to nowhere; back to the box, back to 6th Street, back to San Julian, blown back, face to face with Santa Ana winds, knives of the night, whipping wildly, trash unsettled, garbage disturbed, sounds abridged, sirens silenced, drowned out by blowing air, missing both the treble and the bass.

Bekah and I huddle in unfriendly doorways until dawn breaks, unbroken, into the random unanimous night.

We All Fall Down

If wounds are open, so is time;

If time is open, so are wounds —

Wounds unhealed, battlefield casualties;

Predators stalk when the sun goes down,

Muscles contracting in sinewed night;

We all fall down.

Atoms collide in large geography

Across the soul of Europe;

Ravaged in monastic garments,

So 11th century —

I can't stand the winds;

Mostly it's the noise,

Life's fringes screaming,

Simultaneity realized beneath a crescent moon;

I watch the crows watch the doves,

And vice versa;

Bekah's hands are bigger than mine,

I know because we held our palms together,

Once when we first met:

I had a fifth of decent bourbon

Stuffed in my jacket pocket

Back when I was not so broke —

What do they call it? —

Busted flat,

Bankrupt,

Out of cash,

Overdraft,

Overdrawn,

Cancelled in the first place,

Unbanked,

Pockets empty:

Then, not now

Me and Bekah,

Drinking whiskey,

Walking down Central Avenue,

Cross street Olympic,

Piñatas and carnival barkers,

Helium balloons,

Car stereos installed on the east-west streets,

Blaring hip-hop

For purposes of attraction,

Joining humanity in open time signatures,

I don't hear "Blue Rondo a la Turk,"

But I hear what I want to hear.

I take Bekah's hand as we cross the street,

Wide with many lanes,

To eat bacon biscuits at McDonald's.

My Time with Bekah

Bags

Blow

In

Winds

Scurrying

Like

Squirrels

While

I

Watch

Whales

Off

The

Harbor

San Pedro

Boxes

Unloaded

Into

Trucks

Bound

For the 710

Freeway

I

Don't know

How

I

Got here.

Ice

Watches

Over

Value

Withstood

In

Jewelry

Shopworn

Undescribed

Postulated

In

Pentameter

Discussed

By

Dead men.

Bekah's

Tits

Barely

Sag

Sunsets

Fall

Like

Bombs

Dropped

Old- school

From

Planes

Like Hiroshima

And Nagasaki

65 years

Gone by

Like

Rock

Candy

Mountains

I hold

Bekah's hand

My favorite thing

Through boisterous crowds

In crowded lines

To get some food

Fervor lost

Regained

Through pomp and circumstance

Sirens blare

Schizoid shouts

Hip hop starts and stops

Cars stalked

In red green and yellow.

Open casket

Joey died

In

Broad

Daylight

Never on the news

Awful smell

In dead-dog night

It lasts forever

This voiceless thing

Sea tide

Washing over

The helpless breakers,

Broken,

Buffered,

Water always wins

The fight is fixed

We know not what we do.

I watch

The candle

Burn down

To wax

And ember;

Darwin's ships

Confused with Magellan's,

Lost beyond

The Equator

South of life

Squeezing her fingers

Gentle still,

Her grip is stronger

She holds me tighter

Than I possibly can

Ever reciprocate;

It's never over

Not that I know of

My time with Bekah.

Swept

Around dawn the police came and along with them they had trucks from Public Works and they rousted us and they smashed our tents and our boxes and they rounded us up and shoved us against walls and they patted us down, looking for drugs or weapons or whatever else, and they loaded our belongings into the trucks and they carted our stuff away to a dump, to some location, to wherever, never to be seen again.

By noon we'd re-gathered, come together again, those of us remaining, and we tried to reorganize, but we had nothing much left.

Albert's tent was gone and so was Joey's, and all the boxes were gone, including Bekah's, and I couldn't see her anywhere, and I looked around, but she wasn't there, so I asked—I asked Albert and Joey and I asked the people without tents on 2nd Street, and no one seemed to know, until one old woman, dirty and disheveled—yes, of course—came over to me as I was calling Bekah's name and she said the police had arrested her, had taken her away—they'd found drugs or something on her person, that's how she put it—but, anyway, they'd put her in a patrol car and driven off—they drove away with Bekah in the back seat in handcuffs—and I never saw her again.

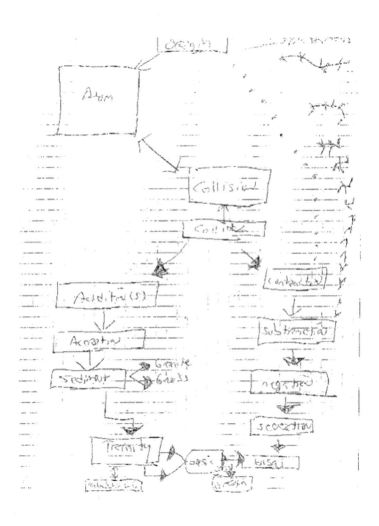

Concluding Rites

Porciuncula

The river that once existed but is no more is the place where the settlers settled. Indians, half Mexicans, African men and women put down their roots. Gunshots riddled the early streets. Then as now.

Lush greenery at the riverbank, now dry. Helicopters swoop on rainy days to rescue kids gone awry—famous on the 11 o'clock news.

Didion's winds still cause madness. Hordes of citizens watch their houses aflame.

History sweeps the sidewalk of soot.

Mickey Cohen nights ring the church bells—all the good citizens still hungry for more.

Skid Row shops festive with trash. Shoptalk standing still at the corner of 6th and San Julian.

Juan Crespi; Fletcher Bowron; Harrison Gray Otis; Pio Pico; Roy Campanella; Clarence Darrow: Dick Riordan; Tom Bradley; John Fante; Francisco Nunez de Balboa; Jerry Brown; Rodney King; Reginald Denny; Daryl Gates: Marvin Gaye; Edward Roybal; the Reverend Cecil Murray; Junipero Serra...

The dam broke and people drowned—no matter what they say.

Adobes built and burnt...The Avila house, one dollar admission...Time lost; time created; space made, space destroyed... Go ahead and tear down my tent, motherfucker!!!

Reflections of the River

I look at the empty river, dry and broken, still in its own way the lifeblood of my city, the place where we hold hands, Bekah and me, the shadows of Narcissus, scattered image, shouting back at me, from the reflections of our history, the refractions of the dark matter, the everything of us all, water rushing past water, petroglyphs remain, time outruns time, fossils fragment never more; sediments rising—no, rising up, rock piling upon rock, dead upon dead, vertebrate and non-vertebrate, sharks' teeth and petrified wood, the Pleistocene and the Holocene.

I don't have a watch; I don't know what time it is, or even what day. Is time running out, or just running on?

The river is a trickle, yet I still see my face in its reflection—Porciuncula refracted in tercentenary faces—Indians, Mexicans, African, Mestizo, our shopping cart voices: Abraham and Isaac, Jacob and Esau, birthrights discarded and revived. I gather belongings, both ordered and scattered, along my Rio Seco, desiccated and alone. I will find my Bekah, if not today, then tomorrow.

The Ending of a Time is the Longest Distance

The river disappears, lost in history and shadows;

The angels seem long gone:

Vanished and vanquished,

Just like me.

It was one place; now it's another place.

Even if I never find you, we will always have what we once had:

Again; not again.

Never again; begin again.

Epilogue

I move from here to there.

Nothing ever ends.

Coda

Except for the river, I have a home no more.

About the Author

Larry Fondation is the author of five books of fiction, all set primarily in the Los Angeles inner city. Three of his books are illustrated by London-based artist Kate Ruth. He has written for publications as diverse as *Flaunt Magazine*, the *Los Angeles Times*, *Fiction International* and the *Harvard Business Review*. He is a recipient of a Christopher Isherwood Fiction Fellowship. In French translation, his work was nominated for SNCF's 2013 Prix du Polar.

CPSIA information can be obtained
at www.ICGtesting.com
Printed in the USA
FSHW01n0528180818
51393FS

9 781947 879010